At Last

by

Susan Vaughan

Devlin Security Force, Protecting Priceless Treasures, Book 4

At Last

Cover Art by *Kim Mendoza*

The Wild Rose Press, Inc.
PO Box 708
Adams Basin, NY 14410-0708
Visit us at www.thewildrosepress.com

Publishing History
First Edition, 2023
Trade Paperback ISBN 978-1-5092-5077-6
Digital ISBN 978-1-5092-5076-9

Devlin Security Force, Protecting Priceless Treasures, Book 4
Published in the United States of America
Previously Published Gullwood Press 2016

Andie looked away from the pleading in his eyes. "Protocol I get. You explained, so you can leave now."

Mike released her, but not touching, kept her in the circle of his arms. Before she could scoot away, he clasped her hands.

"Yes, I had to go, and I was pissed I had to leave you. I'm sorry."

Whoa, a man actually saying the word sorry? A first. The sincerity in his eyes and the warmth of his hands cooled the toxic stew of resentment inside.

She understood his feelings only too well. And she needed to remember she was no longer an impotent kid whose only recourse was rebellion.

"I was furious you ordered me around like some men in my life, but I get your frustration." She squeezed his hands and felt them relax.

Besides, whatever was between them was just for now. He didn't know her, really know her or what she'd done, what she'd been.

"So will you have to run off to put out another fire?" She swallowed, hoping she sounded indifferent.

His arms wrapped around her and heat simmered in his eyes. "I'm off duty. The only fire I'm interested in is right here." Mike lowered his mouth to hers, and the pressure of his lips made her senses reel. The rasp of his beard stubble turned her insides to melted marshmallow.

Dedication

To my loyal newsletter subscribers, who voted to choose the couple for whose wedding this novella this would be. Thanks loads, friends.

Chapter One

ANDIE DEVLIN SLIPPED off her high-heeled sandals and wriggled her toes in the grass. "If the wedding takes as long as this rehearsal—which was *endless*—I'll need to wear lower heels." She flung out her arms, embracing the enormous wedding tent sprawled beside the Severn River.

Cleo Chandler continued walking up the manicured lawn toward the hundred-year-old Riverside Inn where the rehearsal dinner would take place. "My head reels. Mom and Felicity cannot leave things alone, even the schedule the wedding planner guided us through. That must've been the ninetieth time they wrangled details."

Andie frowned at her friend's bunched shoulder muscles, revealed by her strappy cocktail dress. Cleo had been wound for the past few weeks. More photos on the wedding website. Finishing the wedding favors, which she was painting. Final wording on the program. The biggest problem was keeping it "real." Sister-in-law Felicity and Cleo's mom tended toward the princess-fantasy wedding. So not Cleo. As Super Maid of Honor, Andie had stepped up to mediate—also an opportunity to apply her social-work training—but all the hoopla was getting to her too. Neither one needed the added confusion and chaos, not after what they'd been through eight months ago.

Cleo stopped and glanced back at the white tent

where Andie's brother stood in deep conversation with his best man, Lucas Del Rio, and the Navy chaplain, best bud of Cleo's admiral dad at the U.S. Naval Academy. Love glowed in her gaze and softened the curve of her mouth.

An ache tightened Andie's chest. Someday she wanted to have that kind of love, and the same trust and companionship they shared. As if a happily-ever-after was possible for her. *No pity party, like the doc says, Andrea.*

She squinted toward the knot of men, but no way she could read their lips from this far. After the push-pull between the Chandler women, maybe Thomas was smoothing ruffled epaulets. But his stony expression didn't fit that scenario. What was up? Giving orders then, knowing him. She snorted. Even if a forever relationship were possible for her, it wouldn't be with a bossy man like her brother.

She slipped her sandals back on and caught up to Cleo, who had walked ahead, and linked arms with her.

"Whatever they come up with, don't let them change anything now," her friend went on. "Nothing—I repeat, *nothing* must go wrong on my wedding day."

"Hah, nothing *will* go wrong. I won't allow it. This is going to be a perfect wedding, and you'll be the most perfect bride." A perfect wedding, the least she could do for Thomas and Cleo.

"I don't know about perfect, but this suits me a whole lot better than the full-dress military wedding at Annapolis that Dad envisioned."

Andie recalled the time Cleo's father dragged her to a Navy recruitment lecture. "We'd *both* break out in hives."

A vehement shake of the head swept her friend's auburn hair across her shoulders. "I'd have persuaded Thomas to elope."

"And cheat me out of supporting my BFF when she marries my big brother?"

Cleo's laugh eased Andie's tension. As they made their way toward the sedate inn's wide veranda that led to the ballroom, they chatted about whether the toasts after the meal would be just that, or roasts. Andie played coy about what she planned.

Cleo stopped their progress and placed both hands on Andie's shoulders. "Will you be all right? I mean, with all the alcohol swirling around this dinner and almost everything tomorrow?"

"If you'd asked me that question two years ago, I'd say I couldn't handle it. But now, piece of cake. No, make that wedding cake. You're the one under pressure this weekend, not me. As long as the servers have plenty of sweet tea, I'll be golden." She counted on the person who'd known her almost as long as Thomas to see the conviction in her eyes.

Cleo held her gaze a long minute, then nodded. "Anyone hassles you about what you're drinking, remember I have your back. But it turns out sweet tea is a specialty of the inn, both with and without alcohol." She fist-tapped the butterfly tattoo banding Andie's wrist.

Andie tapped the identical design on Cleo's upper arm, and the two hugged.

"Come on up, you lazies. Mom can't find all the place cards." Cleo's look-alike cousin, also a bridesmaid, waved from the veranda. Mimi Ingram lived in Toronto, and the two had met in person those eight months ago, only hours before the smugglers' pursuit that nearly killed them all.

Cleo returned the wave. Then she nudged Andie. "On the veranda, isn't that—?"

Andie followed her gaze. Her heart thumped. "Mike Pagano."

No mistaking that taut body and the black hair in a sexy Marine buzz. In his usual jeans and black tee, he floated her boat, but damn, in tailored pants and a sport coat—both black—he rocked her in waves of heat. He pushed away from the pillar where he'd been lounging.

What the hell was Devlin Security Force's sexiest operative doing *here*?

"You didn't mention he was your date for the weekend." Cleo huffed. "Heck, it's about time. You've been dancing around each other ever since Vegas. I thought you two would never get together."

Andie shook away the fog in her head. "We haven't. I mean, he's not my date."

"He looks yummy. The guy has a thing for you, hon. Give yourself a chance."

Andie barely registered Cleo's departure. She could only stare as Mike descended the three steps and approached.

When he reached her, she lifted her chin and waited. Let him speak first.

Gray eyes framed by dark lashes and thick brows eyed her up and down. Beneath the linen jacket, a silk tee that matched his eyes molded his pecs so perfectly she had to tighten her hands into fists. Damn the man for being so hot.

"Hi, Andie. Bet you're surprised to see me." His voice, smooth and mellow, a little smoky, rippled through her. One side of his mouth ticked up in that small grin that curled her toes.

Her newly manicured nails bit into her palms. The prick of pain freed her power of speech, and she hiked a hand on one hip. "I didn't see your name on the guest list. Looks like you're crashing my brother's rehearsal dinner. And the wedding?" She congratulated herself on her light tone.

"Not crashing anything. I'm working. I'm supposed to hang around all weekend like I'm a guest, me and a few other DSF people. Keep an eye out for trouble."

She gaped. "Devlin Security Force guarding a wedding? What kind of trouble? A wedding-gift thief?"

"A possibility. The inn has nearly two hundred rooms and suites. Too many guests the office had no time to check. Their rent-a-cop will keep an eye out, but he's just one man. Mr. Devlin wanted professionals because of all the brass, the families. You and Cleo. You know how your brother is. Mr. Security." One shoulder lifted in a dismissive shrug.

She studied his expression and saw no hint of dissembling. But even for Thomas, positioning his operatives here seemed over the top. "Maybe."

As she started to sidestep him and walk on, his arm shot out. His grip on her wrist was gentle, but unyielding, his hand rough on her skin, and so warm and tempting she had to bite back a sigh.

"Andie, while I'm here, maybe we can talk. Maybe I can buy y'all a sweet tea later."

She clapped her free hand over one ear. "Ow, ow, ow, Boston. Never again mangle my South Carolina *y'all*."

But jeez, he remembered what she drank.

"Knew I'd get *you* to say it. Turns me on every time." He grinned, and his wink jazzed her pulse. "Come on, live on the edge a little. Sharing a drink can't do any harm."

Except his attitude suggested more than tea. Too macho, too take charge, too much her brother's operative. All reasons to keep her distance.

"The edge? I lived on the edge for way too long." Even fell over the cliff. But she'd revealed enough. "Here's the thing, Mike. On the off chance a thief does try to cart off the gifts, you'll need to be on guard, and I need to make sure this wedding goes off without a hitch."

"Hey, we might find a moment or two."

She stiffened. "Unlikely you've forgotten Vegas, but a reminder can't hurt. Cleo risked her life for me, and so did my brother. You're here to protect everyone and the gifts. So, *y'all*, please see that there's no trouble."

She stared at the masculine hand banding her tattoo. "Count on me."

His fingers slipped away, and dammit, she wanted to cover the spot to seal in his heat. He stepped aside, and she sensed his gaze on her back as she hurried to the veranda.

****

Mike rubbed his nape. *That went well.* Why the hell did Devlin put him in this no-win situation?

He watched her stalk up the lawn, the short red dress swishing against her long legs. No longer short and spiky, her dark-honey hair now brushed her shoulders, but she'd kept the streak of bright color—tonight the same poster-paint blue as her eyes.

After she disappeared safely into the inn, he paced a tight circle. He adjusted his jacket where the lining had caught on the handle of his small 9mm. The first time he'd laid eyes on Andie, that night eight months ago when he was part of Devlin's team that rescued her, he'd wanted her. Her fighting spirit and ability to bounce back—not to mention her sassy looks and kickass bod—turned him on then.

And, man, her mama-tiger attitude turned him on now. More depth to her than he'd realized. Did she know about the threat, or was she just reacting to his clumsy charm offensive? She was attracted but fighting it. Why, he couldn't tell. Unless it was the same reason as his—he worked for her brother. He shook his head. Nah, it was something more than that.

"My little sister give you a hard time?"

Mike pivoted toward the deep voice. He had to look up to meet his boss's gaze. Eyes the same blue as Andie's—eagle fierce instead of sexy—said he'd better not screw up protecting her. Did Thomas Devlin know how Mike felt about her?

Sweat prickled the back of his neck but he managed a grin. "Sir. She always does. I do like a challenge." His peripheral vision caught the smirk on Lucas Del Rio's scarred face as he passed them on the way to the inn. The big DSF operative had already ragged on him about his tough wedding duty.

"I just put the chaplain in the loop." Devlin's expression and stance relaxed, likely in case any of the women were watching. "A bit more intel from the snitch. It's definitely the art theft ring suspected in the Centre Street Museum heist. The nature of the threat is still unclear, but they've killed before. The target could be me or anyone in my family."

Hired by the insurance company, DSF had made the

Baltimore case high priority. The art thieves' Mafia ties ratcheted up the stakes. The thought made him sweat harder. "The FBI any closer?"

Devlin scoffed. "No word on that. Just remember this bunch is ruthless. People are working on stopping the threat to us before any of the guests—and especially the women—suspect there's anything to fear."

"If I notice anything, I'll report in."

"Yeah, but you know your priority."

"Count on me, sir." Pure torture, being close to Andie. And keeping secret the reason.

If she got wind of the plot because he let too much slip, bad news for him. Worst-case scenario, if anything happened to *her*, Devlin would have his ass on a platter.

And Mike would deliver himself to the slaughter.

Chapter Two

ANDIE STOPPED INSIDE the ballroom door to catch her breath. Heck, to locate the air sucked out of the universe. She uncurled her fists and flexed her fingers. Focusing on the polished floor, she swallowed and drew in badly needed oxygen, breathing in and out deeply and slowly, counting her breaths and using the calming technique her therapist had taught her.

What was it about Mike Pagano that flustered her so? Beyond flustered, dammit, and way too affected by his direct gaze. Hotness personified, but it was more. He made her laugh, even with the lame teasing. His cool attitude, like he didn't care what others thought, made her wish she could be more confident. Of course, he didn't have her baggage hanging on his back.

Her date for the weekend? Not likely.

On another deep breath, she looked up and banished Mike from her mind—and other parts—while she let the happy chatter and clink of glasses envelop her. A man's booming laugh echoed in the rafters. Cleo's dad wasn't nicknamed Hoot for nothing.

Although Thomas and their dad were paying for tonight's festivities, Andie reckoned she was the one on the spot if there was a glitch. She weaved her way among relatives and members of the wedding party chatting over drinks. The current group occupied only half the ballroom tonight, but it would be filled to capacity at tomorrow evening's reception. Too big a crowd to suit her.

She rounded the appetizer table piled with shrimp, dips, veggies, cheeses, crackers, and some other, unidentifiable tidbits. She hooked a couple of crackers into the crab dip and whisked away toward Cleo.

Backs to the bar, Cleo and Mimi were nodding and smiling in the direction of the six or so tables. A wedding planner had helped organize the wedding events beforehand, but during the weekend itself, Trudy Ingram, Mimi's mom, was helping out with details. At the moment she didn't look happy.

Maybe because place cards sat only on the head table for the bridal party, none anywhere else.

"Mom, it's no big deal, eh?" Mimi was saying. "It doesn't matter who sits where."

Andie grinned. Seating crisis averted. *Please, let it be the only crisis.*

Irene Chandler joined them, a thick folder and several highlighters cradled in one arm. She tunneled fingers in her hair, shorter and a lighter auburn than her daughter Cleo's. "Here are the schedules for tomorrow. Enough copies for everyone in the wedding party."

Ack, schedules. Like Cleo, Andie hated being boxed in, but for this affair, she conceded the necessity. And the need to step in for the frazzled woman who'd mothered her after hers died.

Before Andie could offer to help label the schedules, Irene gathered up Mimi and Trudy for the job, and the three hurried to a side table.

"Uh oh, blonde on the march," Andie whispered to Cleo.

Felicity was headed toward the women marking the schedules, with that critical expression Andie was coming to know only too well. Cleo's sister-in-law, married to her brother Keith, had picked apart every detail so far. Her ire was partially because she wasn't chosen as matron of honor, Cleo had confided.

"Let Mom handle this. The place card problem was enough." At Andie's raised brow, Cleo giggled. "Tomorrow will be formal. Tonight should be for fun. Besides, a little confusion now might lighten things tomorrow."

Andie let Cleo tug her toward the bar, where the wedding rehearsal crowd was keeping two bartenders busy. *No stress, remember?* Counseling families of troubled teens every day was more stressful than the shock of seeing Mike and dealing with the bridesmaid from hell. She'd focus on just having fun, like her BFF said.

"What'll you lovely ladies have?" The bartender placed drink napkins in front of them. "The wedding special is a Bridal Strawberry. That's berries marinated in strawberry liqueur and served in a flute of Prosecco. Can I pour two?"

Andie backed away slightly while Cleo ordered the special. Older than her, closer to Thomas's age, the barman had green eyes and a drool-worthy chin cleft. He'd dressed to impress in a Riverside Inn polo a size too small that displayed his biceps. Hot, but no Mike Pagano.

Damn, instead of thinking about Mike, she ought to hit on this guy.

She glanced at his brass ID and sent him a smile. "I'll have a sweet tea, Steve. I understand that's y'all's other special."

He grinned. "It sure is. Can I put anything in that besides tea?"

Pushing alcohol on her? No, he was just flirting back. She mustered a wider smile. "Ice cubes, hon."

A moment later, drinks in hand, she and Cleo moved out of earshot.

"Now, finally, we're not surrounded," Cleo said. "How'd your little chat with Mike go?"

Andie told her what he'd said about DSF operatives hanging out during the wedding weekend. "Seems bogus."

Cleo shrugged. "Thomas is concerned about drunken inn guests, others from the bar down the road. Having his people here made sense to me. I didn't know Mike specifically would be here. They all get free rooms and meals."

"Hazard pay?"

They laughed and clinked glasses.

Cleo wrinkled her nose at the first sip of her drink. "Too sweet. I'll stick to Chardonnay after this. So, other than revealing his hazardous duty, what did Mike want?"

"Short answer, he hit on me. Offered to buy me a sweet tea. Wants—" What could she say? "Um, he said he wanted us to talk."

"Sweetie, he wants more than talk. You've talked and teased and bantered at the company Christmas party and at cookouts, but you have a whole weekend here. So what about Mike? Why not see where things might go?"

"There you are. My two favorite babes." Interrupting their conversation, Thomas hooked an arm around his fiancée and bent her backward for a long and noisy kiss.

When Andie had first seen them kiss—and with such obvious love and affection—it had set her back. Even made her blush. But kissing in front of her didn't faze them. Her big brother and her BFF since childhood? Now she knew a mushy smile was curving her lips. She wouldn't even nail Thomas for that *babes* remark.

To give them a moment, she stepped away and looked out the open door onto the veranda. The overhead light shone on a man leaning against a column. A familiar profile, dark clothing, strong features. Her breath caught and gooseflesh danced up her bare arms. He turned his head and looked at her.

"So what about Mike?" What indeed?

****

Standing in the shadows, deeper now that night had fallen, Mike peered through the lounge window. A guy in a gray windbreaker sat at the bar with a half-eaten burger in front of him. Late forties, maybe a little older. Average looks, average height, brown hair. Nothing remarkable, but that was what waved red flags. In constant motion too—tapping his fingers, jiggling one leg, then the other.

Satisfied twitchy guy was settled for a while, Mike texted another operative to watch the guy. He stretched and returned to his original post on the veranda where he could observe Andie. Maybe she was done hitting on the bartender, a sleazy player who probably checked out himself in every mirror he passed.

Mike stretched, loosened his shoulder muscles. Why the hell should he let who she flirted with bother him?

As if his thoughts summoned her, the screen door to the ballroom opened and out she came. She stretched, a move that tightened her sundress top and gave him a prime view of pouty nipples pressing against the thin cloth. His blood heated, and he stepped closer like he was wired to her.

"Everything okay?" Damn. Maybe he should have cleared his throat, or something. He probably scared her. He hauled his gaze upward.

No startle reaction. Instead, she tilted her head and aimed a cool blue stare his way. "You still out here?"

Another question was not an answer. Interesting. "Still at my post, ma'am. Keeping an eye out, as instructed by you."

"And my brother. But don't you get time off for good behavior? I mean, you have to eat sometime."

He slapped one hand over his heart and lifted his gaze to the heavens. "Ah, she cares."

"Don't get too excited. Cleo said you and the others get room and board during this gig. I spotted Brickley— y'all call him Brick, right, cause he's kinda shaped like one?—and another guy chowing down in the bar earlier. Not you."

"So you were looking for me? See, you do care."

Eye roll. Big sigh.

"Okay, I'll let you off the hook. Brick spelled me out here while I ate, not bar food. But in the dining room, where they serve crab cakes. Not the same as in Boston, but damned good."

The twitchy guy came back out. Sat on a wicker rocking chair and lit a cigarette. Maybe he was a bored salesman or waiting for somebody, and maybe that bulge under his jacket was a paperback and not a gun. Or maybe Mike was too damned suspicious. Hell, he was paid to be suspicious. Especially now. And it didn't hurt that Brick had noticed the guy too.

"Nice and quiet out here," Mike said, "but not in there. Hard to hear the music over the chatter."

A woman at an electronic piano and a man with an acoustic guitar had been tickling out oldies for a while. "Isn't She Lovely?" was the song playing at the moment.

Whoo boy, yeah.

"Hard to blame them. A lot of the relatives haven't seen each other in a long time. Cleo was in Europe for a few years, so she has a lot of catching up. The aunts and uncles are mobbing her. Too much of a mob. I needed to escape."

"I get that. I'm not big on crowds myself." He tugged on one ear. "I'd rather have you all to myself." And away from that bartender. Hell, the guy was just doing his job pushing drinks. "Hard to hear much of the toasts out here. Whatever you said resulted in a lot of laughter and some soaked tissues. I caught only a few words. Wish I'd heard more."

She shrugged as if it didn't matter, but color rose in her cheeks. "When Cleo and I were kids, her brothers and mine let us trail after them. I reckon they babysat us some too. We played pranks on them and vice versa. I shared a few of the more interesting ones."

"Any about Cleo and your brother?" He stroked an imaginary goatee.

"Forget using any of what I know to push for a raise. Tommy would just laugh."

"Tommy?" Sure didn't suit the man who ran DSF. Although, he was a different man around Cleo. More relaxed, less ex-Delta.

"Until he went into the Army, he was Tommy. I still call him that sometimes."

"Crazy kid stuff wouldn't drive people to tears," he

said. "What else? What you said this afternoon about them risking their lives for you?"

Her open expression shuttered. "That was it. And how important both of them are to me. My two most fave people in the world."

Twitchy guy left his seat and ambled closer. Too close to Andie. From where the guy stood, he could see into the ballroom through one of the open windows. Could be nothing. Could be something. But Andie was Mike's priority.

He took her hand and drew her away into the shadows. No one else there except a couple on a loveseat farther down the veranda. "They're playing our song. Dance with me."

She let him take her in his arms and twirl her in circles. She felt soft in all the right places, yet strong. No delicate miss, though her light scent, some kind of flower, made him want to bury his nose in her hair. He kept hold of her hand and held her close but in the traditional dance position. After a few twirls, her left hand came to rest on his shoulder. No rebellion yet. He'd see where this went.

"What *is* our song?" Her voice, close to his ear, was breathy, husky. And damn, they fit together. In heels, she was nearly his height.

"A very old oldie. 'Dancing in the Dark.'"

She huffed. "Not the Rihanna song, for sure."

"Not Springsteen either. This is the original." *Like you.* Original, a bit of a rebel, and fiercely loyal to those she loved. He turned her for a better angle on twitchy guy, but the man had disappeared. Mike would text Brick later. He sang along until the pianist took off into a jazzier version.

"You even know the words. You must be older than I thought. Where are your cane and hearing aid?"

"By cracky, I'm only thirty-four," he said in his best geezer imitation. When she laughed, he eased her closer for a better whiff of her scent.

"Let's see." She gazed thoughtfully up at the ceiling. "Thomas sent you undercover in an oldies band. No, that's not it. You're a fan of old black-and-white films." She wrinkled her nose. "Aha, I have it. Your family forced you to perform musicals in stock theater, and you escaped into the Marines. You're a Jarhead and not Delta, so that's why he sent you to the oldies band."

"Nope. It's because I keep humming those retro songs." He lifted her captured hand so he could kiss the pulse point on the inside of her wrist. But she resisted his effort at turning it over, and instead his lips found the little inked butterflies on the back. "Number three guess almost has it. No band op, but as a Jarhead, I had to prove myself."

"So, the song?" she prompted, a little breathless.

Good. Maybe she'd welcome other kisses. "You have my great-grandmother Rossi to thank for your musical entertainment. She taught piano for years. When I was in elementary school, my brother and my cousins and I all went to her house after school because our parents worked." Hell, not his dad, but he wasn't going there. "Nonna played songs from the forties and fifties, and we sang along. You play a few bars of any song from then, I bet you I can sing the lyrics."

"That's so sweet. You were a good kid to sing for her."

"No singing meant no homemade cookies or cake. My cousin Joey refused for a week before he caved."

"But not you? I figured you for the hold-out."

"Nah. I like to sing. Doesn't much matter what."

She looked away, then back at him through lowered lashes. "You have a good voice. I'd like to hear another song."

He'd been listening only to her, not to the music. Not *their* song now, but something slow again, thank the musical gods. He wanted her in his arms.

When she started to step away, he said, "Don't know the words to this one. But if you dance with me, I'll hum."

"Too new?" she teased, but returned to him. She linked her fingers behind his neck. "Don't get any ideas, but it's easier to follow your lead this way."

"I like the sound of that." And the feel of her against him. And the puff of her breath against his cheek.

She tilted her head back and peered at him. "About not getting ideas?"

"That you're eager to follow my lead. And too late, I already have ideas."

Before she could come back with a snappy retort, he kissed her. Her lips parted and her hands gripped his shoulders. She was finally yielding to what had been cooking between them for months. Sweet.

He pulled her closer and deepened the kiss, drinking her in, tea and something tangy—the flavor of Andie. She was kissing him back and swirling her tongue against his. He skimmed his fingers through her hair, down the frantic pulse in her throat. The taste of her steamed his blood and sent it south. He swelled and hardened in the kind of frantic rush he hadn't experienced since his horny teens. He burned for her, and his body hummed.

"Andie," he murmured, "let's—"

Alertness finally penetrated the haze in his brain. The humming wasn't his body.

He dragged his mouth from her lips. "Sorry, sorry. My phone. It's, damn." Unable to formulate a coherent explanation, he snatched the vibrating devil from his pocket.

She let go and stepped back, and the loss felt more than physical. One hand flew to her mouth. Best not to wonder if she was savoring his taste or wiping him away. She looked as dazed and confused as he felt.

He held up the phone. Brick. He had to answer. "M.P. here. Yeah?"

The call had stopped him from taking things too far, too fast. And in public. But… damn.

Chapter Three

ANDIE SHOOK HER head, her brain stuttering to life even as a fever raged in her body. *"What about Mike?"* Cleo could've had no idea her question would ignite such flames.

Andie'd wanted to know what kissing Mike would be like, and she found out big time. He was heat and man and need. And he roused the same need in her, pure molten and racing through her veins. They'd been so close she felt the muscles in his legs and the solid bulge between them. He kissed her with thoroughness, his mouth so hot and hungry she practically climbed up his hard body to get closer.

If only his fingers had kept working their magic lower to where her breasts ached for his touch. But the phone call jerked them apart.

Jeez, was she so hard up she would do it on a darkened porch? She'd cut off the guys from her past as bad news. Since sobering up, she'd focused on building a future, so she hadn't been with anyone. Hadn't dared, hadn't wanted.

Until tonight. An invisible wire of attraction had pulled them together. As they danced, he held her with firm but gentle control and sang to her. She was adrift in sensation—the steady beat of his heart against her breast, the warmth of his breath against her cheek. Then when he told her about his grandmother, how could she not completely melt? They'd almost moved and breathed as one.

She'd held herself at a distance with controlled numbness for so long that the lush sensations surprised her. The chemistry between them set her hormones into overdrive, but it wasn't just the sizzle. He was a solid and steady guy, but fun to be with. No one kidded with her and made her laugh like Mike.

He stood at the veranda's edge, turned away and hunched over his phone, all broad shoulders and intensity as he listened and replied in low tones.

Now he faced her and stuffed the phone into his pocket. He stepped closer, stopping only a hand's breadth away. Did he mean to pick up where they left off? Her pulse took off again and her lips parted.

Dragging fingers through his inky hair, he looked left, then right toward the veranda's shadowy recesses.

Before she could ask if he was checking for spectators, he said, "Duty calls. Catch you later."

Her ears rang with the dismissal. She knew this song all too well. Had heard it all through her fractured childhood. She lifted a shoulder as if she didn't give a rip. "Maybe."

"Go back inside to the party," he growled, his face set in stone, "and stay there."

The sharp command sliced through her and her cheeks burned. She glared.

He stared back.

To end the glare/stare contest, she stepped inside. When she turned around to tell him to go to hell, he'd vanished into the night.

Her stomach curled in on itself, and she pressed her

fingertips to her lips, still damp and swollen from his kisses. She should've known. He finally showed his true, arrogant colors. Domineering. High-handed. Like her brother, like her dad, giving orders.

The combo began the next tune—"It's in his Kiss." Damn, that was the problem, wasn't it? His kiss, her new drug of choice. *Ouch.* Take a chance on him? It would never work. The arrogance, she could handle, but if he knew her, knew her past... She turned away from the music.

Go inside and stay there? Not likely. Andie kicked off her sandals and stomped outside and onto the lawn. Maybe the night air would cool the heat simmering inside her. She wandered down toward the wedding tent, where she could sit on one of the folding chairs and put her feet up. A tiny red glow inside alerted her to a smoker's presence. Not in the mood for company, she veered away along the riverbank, the only place to go unless she returned to the inn. A lazy quack drifted up from the river along with the smell of water and the tang of mud.

So duty called, did it? Even if that was true, Mike didn't have to shoo her away like a child. He might as well have patted her on the head. Cleo would tell her it was no big deal, that he was just protecting her in case some other guy came out to hit on her. Yeah, yeah, all that protective shtick, it was embedded in their DNA, men like him. Protect her from some other guy coming out to hit on her? Like that would happen.

Chill, Andrea. She stopped at the inn's dock, where the admiral's cabin cruiser and a sailboat rocked beneath pole lights. One of the DSF operatives stood nearby, on his phone.

Then the rangy man stowed the phone and hustled off the dock, stopping short when he spied her. A wide smile split his brown face. "Hey, Andie."

"Hey, Hakim. Problem with the *Prowler*?"

He grinned. "Looks damn good to me. I'd like one of those."

"Who wouldn't?" Snowy-white, sleek, and powerful, with all the amenities. She lifted an eyebrow.

"Nothing's wrong. Mr. D asked me to see if he'd left it unlocked. He didn't." He stowed his phone. "Thought you were at the party. Everything okay?"

She flicked a wave and smiled. "Just perfect. You guys are busy tonight. What's up?"

But he'd already jogged away. Like Mike.

Just as well. She'd used up all her snappy repartee for the evening. She strolled toward her dad's baby, scuffing her bare feet on the dock until the thought of a splinter prompted more careful steps. The fifty-footer rocked gently, tied fore and aft to sturdy bollards.

Tomorrow after the reception, Thomas and Cleo would sail off on their honeymoon cruise. Neither would say exactly where on the Chesapeake. "Oh, wherever the tide takes us," Cleo had said. Thomas would say nothing. Typical.

But not typical of their old man to offer anyone, even his responsible son, use of the *Prowler*. Was her dad mellowing in his old age? In his relationship with Thomas, maybe, but so far not with her.

Footsteps crunched on the gravel path. A man, far enough away from the light she couldn't see him well enough to tell if he was part of the wedding or one of the DSF guys.

Could she not get away from people?

The man halted and jogged back up the lawn. Apparently he didn't want company either. Or he forgot something.

Either way, she got what she wanted, peace and quiet. Solitude. Uh-huh.

****

Mike bent and circled the older Jag sedan as he played his phone's flashlight over the tires. No flats, no cut marks. He straightened and stretched his back. By his calculation, he'd been gas-fume close to more upscale cars and SUVs tonight than he had in his whole life. Finished with his section of the inn guest lot, he gave Brick a thumbs-up sign. The stocky veteran operative was in charge of the wedding detail this weekend.

Brick acknowledged him, but continued scuttling along his row. Hakim was working another section. Earlier, a phone app had alerted Thomas Devlin to tampering on his brand-new hybrid SUV.

Brick's phone call had sent Mike here—and away from Andie. He'd called one of the other guys to watch her, but learned other suspicious shit was pulling everybody from their posts. Somebody trying to break into the Devlins' suite. And gunshots behind the kitchens.

Still, he should've told Brick he couldn't leave Andie.

He made his way to the lot's center and leaned against the fender of a silver Cadillac.

Andie. He was an idiot. Worse, an asshole. The craving for her had drained all sense from his brain. Fear that a serious attack was going down erupted from him in barked commands—guaranteed to tick her off. Her cool brush-off was an act. He saw the anger and hurt in her eyes. Coward that he was, he ran off without an explanation. Not that he could've told her anything, true or concocted on the spot.

Shit, he'd be lucky if she listened to an apology. Even luckier if she considered picking up where they left off.

Brick and Hakim joined him by the last sedan. Brick had called in the alert and sent Hakim to check on the admiral's yacht, just in case. Mike, Brick, and two others, who left now to carry out a perimeter check, had converged on Devlin's vehicle to find all four tires slashed and a note beneath one wiper: *"You and yours are next."*

"I got nothing. No slashed tires, no keyed car bodies. Nada." Brick looked to Hakim.

The taller man held up his phone. "Only a dead battery. Next time I bring a separate flashlight."

Brick frowned. "If there's a next time, we use transceivers and earbuds, not smart phones so we blend in."

"So you think this is part of the threat?" Mike asked. "Seems damned petty."

Hakim attached a tiny charger to his smart phone and dumped both in a pocket. "Maybe they intend to wear us out with stupid pranks, lull us into complacency."

"Not a bad theory," Brick said. "Could also be a diversion. The others too."

"To draw us away from the dinner." Mike straightened away from the Caddy. "In that case, it worked."

"We keep this in-house. No cops. Don't want to alarm anyone in the inn, especially the wedding guests."

Brick took out his phone and scrolled. "I know a guy in Severna Park who'll take care of the boss's SUV. It'll be back by morning with four new tires. You two get back to the inn, and I'll fill in Mr. D."

Mike and Hakim hurried past the lobby entrance and around the veranda to the ballroom. Music and conversation still drifted through the open windows.

"I'm assigned to the bar and the lobby. Snooze duty. I'll need strong coffee," Hakim said when they reached the doorway. "One of the other guys'll be on the lookout for the sketchy character you noticed."

Mike glanced both directions. "No sign of him now."

"See you later." Hakim grinned. "You have the prime gig—Andie Devlin."

Mike winced at the prospect of facing her. How the hell would he explain? As he crossed to the ballroom door, he checked his phone screen for the GPS tracker her brother had inserted in her phone. The blip showed her down by the river.

He tensed and the hairs rose on his nape. He spun back. "Damn, she didn't stay put."

At what must be shock on his face, the other operative held up his hands. "Hey, I thought you knew, man. I saw her at the dock."

Mike took off like a greyhound after a rabbit.

****

After cooling her heels, literally, and toes in the river, Andie retrieved her dad's hidden key and opened the storage beneath the seats. Collecting a couple of cushions and a blanket, she settled in the cockpit. Her phone read eight-fifteen. Crap, she was sitting here alone when she could've been getting to know Mimi and her mom better. Cleo probably wondered about her. Even Thomas.

Bright lights and laughter beat sitting here feeding her resentment. If that's what she felt. Where was the doc when she needed clarity? If not the doc, then a chat with her roomie, for a different kind of clarity. Her roomie'd been acting odd recently, and before Andie left this morning, Erin had slammed out the door without a word. She tapped the number, but the call went to voice mail. Finding out what was going on would have to wait. Crap.

The sound of feet pounding down the dock shot her to her feet just in time to face their owner, as Mike screeched to a halt. Her foolish heart thrilled into rapid beats. This man tangled up her insides in ways she didn't understand, and all her senses seemed to open to his energy.

She lifted her chin. "You racing to a fire or something?"

Breathing hard, he bent and placed his hands on his knees. "What are you doing... down here... by yourself?"

"Don't you have anything better to do than frighten people who just want to be left alone?"

"Don't *you* know... people are worr- wondering about you?" His breathing appeared to regulate, and he straightened.

"Why is it any of your business?" She couldn't make herself stop challenging him, forcing the issue. Even if Cleo had sent him.

"Do you always answer questions with questions?"

"I can keep going if you can." She hugged the oversize sweatshirt she'd unearthed tighter around her. "Until you answer my first question."

One side of his mouth ticked up before a slow smile spread over his face, tracing laugh lines around his wide mouth and making his dark eyes sparkle with mischief.

"My mom says *I'm* stubborn, but you have me beat." He held up his hands in classic surrender, but took a step closer to the boat. "Truce. Okay, I was running because I heard a splash and was afraid you'd fallen in."

That was a lie, well, maybe a tiny fib. She'd heard no splash, but never mind. He was still smiling the smile that made her all soft inside, made her want, a *want* she didn't know if she could resist. She fisted her hands in the folds of the sweatshirt. "I can swim, Pagano, and I've been on boats since I was a baby. So who invited you here?"

"Back to questions, are we?" He planted a rubber-soled shoe on the deck. "Permission to come aboard?"

"I can't stop you, can I?" She backed up as he joined her in the cockpit, which didn't seem as spacious as before.

"Sweet craft." He sleeked a palm along the gunwale as his gaze swept the *Prowler* from bow to stern. "What's she got for power?"

Big whoop, males and motors, just her thing. She resumed her cushioned seat and folded her hands in her lap—loosely, not clenched. "Twin MerCruiser 450's. You know power boats?"

Taking a seat opposite her, he shook his head. "Not much. Only what I learned in the Marines. So what are you doing here?"

"I asked the first question, remember?"

Faster than she could react, he scooted across the deck and joined her on her cushion. "Softer seat over here." He grinned. Again. "As I recall, asked and answered. I thought you might've fallen in. But I'll let you off the hook. Hakim said you were here. I came to explain about earlier."

Her heart raced so hard she could hear its beat in her ears. Take a chance on him or not? "Not necessary. Go away."

"Like hell." His voice was burlap rough, his features tight with male emotion—impatience or frustration or both. "We were all over each other, and now you won't listen to reason. What is it with you, Andie?"

She'd need hours to answer that. Like maybe never. She hiked up a shoulder. "I knew you were on duty. You got a call and had to go. What was that about?"

"It, um…" He raked fingers through his hair, mussing it adorably, dammit. "I told you, DSF operatives are making sure the weekend goes smoothly. To use your terms, we put out a small fire. No big deal."

Her chest tightened. He'd hurt her, and now he was shutting her out *again* in a way she knew all too well. She *only* wanted an answer. "A small fire. Then why—"

"Andie, no matter what happened, I can't break protocol. I'd lose my job." He placed his hands on her shoulders. "Please understand."

She looked away from the pleading in his eyes. Except for his wanting to be honorable about the company, his replies were too rushed, bogus. Something more than simple wedding security was going on. Or she was being too sensitive, too defensive. Not the first time, admittedly.

"Protocol I get. I'll let it go. For now." She ought to brush away his hands, but couldn't make herself move. "You explained, so you can leave now."

He released her shoulders, but without touching,

kept her in the circle of his arms, caging her from escape. Smart man. Before she could scoot away, he clasped her hands.

When she struggled, he held on. "I'm not finished. Yes, I had to go, and I was pissed. Pissed that I had to leave you. And pissed at myself that I resented having to do my job, a job that's important to me. I took out my frustration on you. I'm sorry."

Whoa, a man apologizing, actually saying the word *sorry*? A first. She faced him again. The sincerity in his eyes and the warmth of his hands cooled the toxic stew of resentment and whatever else inside her.

She understood his feelings only too well. And she needed to remember she was no longer an impotent kid whose only recourse was anger and rebellion.

"I was furious you ordered me around like some other men in my life, but I get your frustration." She squeezed his hands and felt them relax.

At the company Christmas party, he'd shared experiences in Afghanistan as an M.P. and told her how DSF had recruited him because his commanding officer knew Thomas. As a take-charge operative and a Marine—once a Marine, always a Marine, never *ex*—he would bark orders again, but she could handle that better next time.

Besides, whatever was between them was just for now. He didn't know her, really know her or what she'd done, what she'd been.

"So will you have to run off to put out *another* fire?" She swallowed, hoping she sounded indifferent.

His arms wrapped around her and heat simmered in his eyes. "I'm off duty. The only fire I'm interested in is right here." Mike lowered his mouth to hers, and the pressure of his lips made her senses reel. The rasp of his beard stubble against her skin turned her insides to melted marshmallow.

When he pulled her closer and deepened the kiss, she let him tug her up so she straddled his lap. She was adrift in sensation, aware only of him, of his strength and his scent—citrus, clean, earthy—and the burgeoning hardness against her, spreading heat into her belly and thighs.

He kissed her with his tongue, his teeth, and seemingly his entire body, melting her very bones, every inch of her body sensitized to him. She yearned toward him as his hand trailed heat down her back and along her thigh.

The night air had chilled her, but she was cooking from the inside, steaming in the heavy cotton. "I have on too many clothes." She yanked the sweatshirt off over her head and tossed it onto the deck. "You too." She slid her hands under the jacket across his shoulders, letting her fingers linger over the heavy muscle and bone.

His hands clamped her wrists. "Andie, stop."

Chapter Four

MIKE FELT HER go still. Dammit, he couldn't let her start stripping him. He knew where that would go. Not doing his duty to protect her would be the least of it.

But now she was going to think he didn't want her. Didn't want her? He craved her with an ache that throbbed through his whole body, but mostly where her sexy little butt was pressed.

Color flared high on her cheeks, and she pulled back. When he released her wrists, her hands fell away, leaving the fizz of her touch.

"Stop?" Her breathy question nearly had him stripping her the rest of the way—except for the wariness in her baby blues and the warning in his head.

He pulled her close again, and she let him. *Oo-rah!* Touching his forehead to hers, he willed his heartbeat to slow from mach speed. "If I'm right about where we were headed, this boat is too public. An open cockpit, a lighted dock."

"And people wandering the grounds. You're right, about both."

As if on cue, a feminine laugh rang out from the wedding tent.

Andie's lips compressed, she turned toward the shuttered companionway. "I knew where to find a key to the cushion storage, but my dad doesn't trust me with the other keys. We can't get inside." Her lips stretched into a grin that looked forced. "Unless you brought an official DSF lock-pick kit."

He snapped his fingers. "Dang, I left mine in my official DSF equipment locker."

She eased off his lap and onto the cushion. "Anyway, maybe we need to cool down."

No shit. If the little voice of reason hadn't reminded him where they were and what he was *supposed* to be doing, they could've been naked and oblivious to everything but the hunger and urgency between them. Good thing she had no keys, or he'd have had to do some fast thinking. The thought of Andie as a prime target, trapped naked below in a bunk with no escape, shrank the last of his erection.

He blew out a breath as he clicked on something she'd said. "No keys? Your old man doesn't trust you with this beast? You even know the horsepower."

"I know this boat inside and out, but Dad doesn't trust me with much." Her face seemed to tighten against her skull, her eyes cooled, and her expression went blank. She looked away and smoothed her dress across her knees, as if she regretted her words. On a shrug, she added, "He's never gotten over my teenage rebellion."

Her forced nonchalance meant a whole lot of baggage weighed down those words. He tucked a blonde strand, silky and sweet smelling, behind her ear. "Is the bright streak part of rebelling?"

"What's left of it. And now Crayola hair color is the fashion. Who knew I was a trend setter?"

"I like the color. A little rebellion's not a bad thing." He grinned. "Did a fair amount of it in my teens too."

Her eyes widened. "You? Mr. Straight-Arrow

33

Marine?"

"Yeah, well, that came later. I ran with a tough crowd until my dad died." When she uttered a little hum of sympathy, he cleared his throat. "Car accident. I was seventeen and had to straighten out fast to help the family."

"I'm so sorry. So you and your mom? Any brothers or sisters?"

"My sister Teresa, three years younger than me, and Danny, a year after her." His throat closed, and he had to look away. Five years later, and he still couldn't talk about Danny. His kid brother, caught in the same trap that killed their dad. Andie's hand on his arm pulled him out of the funk. "When Mr. D hired me, he knew about my dad and told me about the two of you losing your mom. So you've been there."

"Mom had breast cancer. Thomas was fifteen, and I was seven. We had a rocky time afterward, Dad included, although then I was too young to be aware of that. He dived into his work. Duty, stiff upper lip and all that. Cleo's family sort of wrapped Tommy and me in their arms. That propped me up for a few years." She picked up her phone from the cushion beside her. "I keep photos of Mom in here so I don't forget what she looked like."

Suddenly the device began to beep, louder and louder.

"Whoops, the alarm." She shut off the racket. "I set it in case I fell asleep. I need to get back to the party before it's over." She tucked the phone in her small handbag, then carried the sweatshirt across the cockpit and opened the storage hatch.

He collected the cushions and waited while she

stowed everything and locked up. He picked up her heels from the dock and handed them to her. They remained quiet as they strolled up the lawn.

A glance at her profile didn't offer a clue to what she was thinking. Maybe she had the same concerns about keeping things casual between them. His misgivings about a relationship, hell, even a weekend, with Devlin's sister hadn't magically vanished, but spending more time with her stuffed that concern to the back of his mind. She was funny and vulnerable, and a tough babe, and he wanted her. Bad.

How could he walk the tightrope of getting in deeper with her while protecting her? And still lying to her? Shit.

When her shoulders moved in a shiver, he wrapped an arm around her. "Andie, I'm glad we talked."

"Me too. Who'd have thought, us a couple of orphans—partial orphans—and former rebels?" She snuggled closer, a happy smile on her face, and his body swelled. "I still hear music up there. The evening's not over."

A Latin version of "Save the Last Dance for Me" and voices singing along floated from the ballroom.

Hell, they'd almost reached the inn, where Cleo stood on the veranda, and he still couldn't find the right words. Halting, he turned Andie in his arms. "Look, we slowed things down. It doesn't mean we're over, but—"

"'Course not. We have the whole weekend." She flashed him a smile that made her face glow in the moonlight, a smile that promised heat and sensuality, a smile that drained his blood south. "Plenty of time for more dancing."

A brush of soft lips on his and she was gone.

He could only stand there, his body on fire and unsaid intentions crowding his throat, as she hooked arms with her BFF and skipped inside.

****

When Cleo declared she was parched, Andie let her friend steer her to the bar, where the chunky barman whose name she didn't know was whipping up a frozen drink smelling of melons. Ick. When she'd tended bar, mixing those fruity drinks had never tempted her to backslide, which was a good thing.

The barman acknowledged them with a harried nod.

Cleo ordered for them, sweet tea for Andie and club soda for her. "Enough wine for me tonight. Way to go, girlfriend. Looks like you took a chance after all. That was some hot kiss."

"And probably the last." Andie felt sure that Cleo wouldn't press for more yet because of the crowd around them. The other bartender, Steve, came around the corner with a tray of glasses. Cleo's uncle, another naval officer—they were surrounded—called him over, asking something about remembering him tending bar in Annapolis. Andie tuned them out and wound her fingers in her handbag strap.

Judging from Cleo's pursed mouth and thoughtful expression, she'd have to fess up soon, but not until they could find privacy. She relaxed a fraction when Cleo brightened and blew a kiss to Thomas, across the ballroom with her brothers.

A sharp elbow nudged Andie. "Look over there beyond the last table. Lucas and Mimi with their heads together."

Oh good, a neutral topic, another happy couple. Andie tamped down the black hole inside her and pasted on a smile. "They deserve happiness, especially together."

"Thomas says they've been racking up the frequent-flyer miles between D.C. and Toronto. Physical distance is an obstacle, of course, but self-imposed emotional distance is a bigger one."

"Or a *realistic* one?" In Andie's case, distance meant self-protection.

Steve set down two glasses. "Sorry you had to wait, ladies."

Cleo thanked him and tugged Andie toward a table by a potted palm. "So. Now that no one is listening… Last kiss? What I saw didn't look like *The End*."

Andie took the seat facing the exit. No sign of Mike out there. She sipped her tea and felt a chill, and not from the icy liquid. Here was the first guy in forever she could really go for, and it was over before it started. Just as well. The stress of this weekend was enough. All the family to keep happy, wedding details, free alcohol. Not exactly free because Thomas and Cleo's dad were covering, but still.

The musicians had stopped playing and were packing up. The remaining guests clustered at the bar and near the head table, leaving the nearby tables empty of all but empty glasses and crumpled napkins. No eavesdroppers.

She set her tea glass on the table. "You weren't there. He said those breakup code words " she made air quotes with her fingers "—like it was good we talked and we weren't over, but…"

"But what?" Opposite her, Cleo sipped her club soda.

"That's when I kissed him, so I wouldn't have to

hear what came after that, as in 'I love you, but...' His next words would be something like 'let's just be friends.'" She blew out a breath and gulped the last of her drink.

Cleo squeezed her forearm. "You're trying to protect yourself, but all you're doing is cutting yourself off from a great guy. He didn't mean what you think and you didn't let him finish. I saw the dumbstruck look on his face after you kissed him. He couldn't take his eyes off you. I think pole-axed is the scientific term."

Cleo's pep talks usually cheered Andie, but all she could manage now was a tiny tug of her lips. "Yeah, maybe he gets off on kissing me, but he'll kick me to the curb fast enough once he finds out about my past, like all the other guys." When she'd told them about her wild-child years, they either backed off or offered her drugs. She didn't see Mike as the second type.

"Outrageous. Anticipating the kick, you jump off the curb and stretch out on the pavement." Cleo crossed her arms over her chest and wailed, "Oh, come on, y'all just run me over now."

Andie huffed at the southern drawl, which Cleo had mostly left behind. She started to argue, but her friend held up a hand.

"Those guys who ditched you because you were honest—yes, and brave—weren't worth ant spit. You're better than that. Mike is better than that. Thomas is very impressed with him, says he's a leader who'll go far." Cleo's gaze flicked past Andie's shoulder toward the bar. "Why, I bet he'll show up any moment to clear things up."

When a sly smile curved her friend's lips, a tingle crept up Andie's spine. *Mike*. He must've come in through the inn door. "Cleo, don't—"

"You two must be cooking up something." Mike's voice, low and slightly gruff, skated over her nerves. He held two ice-filled glasses. "Can an outsider join you?"

Too late now to beg Cleo not to leave her alone with him. Andie forced herself to meet his gaze, and the sheer intensity there stopped her breath.

Cleo popped up from her seat. "Whoops, my lord and master beckons." She scooted away, leaving in her wake the whiff of matchmaking.

Mike set down the two glasses and moved Cleo's vacated chair beside hers before plopping down. "Thought it was time we shared that sweet tea."

She nodded but couldn't look him in the eye and couldn't come up with anything to say other than the obvious. "Thanks."

"Look, I'm pretty sure I left you with the wrong impression. I'm no whiz with the opposite sex. Explaining myself doesn't come easy, so I fumbled the ball."

No ladies' man, with those bedroom eyes and panther's walk? Not in this lifetime. "You don't have to explain. I get it. You're working this weekend. No biggie." She wedged the words out past the cotton wad in her mouth. A sip of the cold tea helped and gave her something to do with her hands.

But not for long because as soon as she set down the glass he linked fingers with her, sending a little thrill up her arm.

"I don't think you get it at all because I was such an idiot. I like you, Andie, a lot. You're funny and sexy and you don't take any crap from me. And yes, I'm working, but that's not it. I want more with you than behaving like two teens grappling in a backseat—or on a boat cushion. I want more than this wedding weekend."

Something deep inside her eased, but she firmed her resolve. All those shaky years had taught her to operate with her guard up. "That's so sweet. I like you a lot too. Let's enjoy what time we have together this weekend, and then we'll see."

The scent of magnolias and the clatter of high heels announced an arrival. "Don't mean to interrupt y'all, but the admiral just cracked another bottle. Enjoy!" The whirlwind placed two full flutes of champagne before them.

"Thanks, Felicity," Andie said as the other woman floated away on a cloud of perfume. "She's married to Cleo's brother Keith." According to Cleo, their marriage was a happy union, but how that worked was a mystery to Andie.

"That blonde was a woman on a mission." His laugh was a low rumble that shimmered into her. He dumped his bubbly into the potted palm. "I don't care for this stuff. I'll stick with the tea I brought us." Smiling *that* smile, he wrapped his big hand around hers.

"She's a force, all right." But she wasn't aware of Andie's issues. If she had been, she'd probably take advantage. Andie turned and poured her glass into the plant.

His head jerked backward in a double take. "I thought all women liked champagne."

She twisted in her seat, moved her shoulders back and forth. Something the doc had asked once came back to her. Was what she feared waiting to ambush her from the outside, or was it inside her? Her heart knocked to the beat of a hummingbird's wings.

She forced herself to meet his curious gaze. "Sweet tea is more than a preference. I don't drink alcohol or do drugs. Haven't for six years. In recovery and sober for two." She held her breath, waiting for him to withdraw his hand.

His brows crimped, pleating the skin between them, and he squeezed her hand gently but continued to hold it. His gaze was grave but gentle. "You want to tell me about it?"

The tightness in her chest eased, but her nerves prickled. Laying it all out had driven away other guys—and friends.

"It was worse than just rebelling. I couldn't do anything right, and Dad trusted me with nothing. We argued about everything."

"Where was your brother through this?"

"At college and then in the Army. After he left for Special Forces duty, I didn't see him for a long time. Even if he'd been around, I don't know if he could've done anything." Or if anyone could have. They'd moved away from Cleo and her family in South Carolina, to the big city of Washington, D.C., the land of loneliness and temptation.

She shook off the memory of those first days away from her best friend. "It gets worse. Promise just to listen and let me talk." On his nod, she continued. She told him about running away, sometimes sleeping on other kids' couches. About the partying, the binge drinking, the cocaine and marijuana and pills. About ending up on the street, then in jail, and the final deep pit. "I didn't understand until years later, but losing my mom like that caused depression."

Through all this, he held both her hands and stayed

silent, somehow conveying support. His gaze held her, strengthened her, and seemed to block out the chatter around them.

She drew a long breath. "I was twenty-four. Sitting in that cell, I saw no way out except this." She turned over her right hand. Partly camouflaged by her tattooed cuff, the scar winked to the rapid beat of her pulse.

"The reason you wouldn't let me kiss your wrist."

She nodded. "I couldn't even kill myself with the shank I found hidden in my mattress. I bled all over the cot but didn't hit the artery. My cellmate ratted me out, and they sent me to the hospital."

"And your dad?" His voice was rough with emotion.

"Away on his last command. At sea. In more ways than one." Tears burned her throat as she choked out the rest. "Tommy came. I owe him my life. He supported me through rehab and counseling and finishing college. I love my brother, but not his over-protective, high-handed routine. For the next few years, I gave him nothing but attitude and the sharp edge of my tongue until I felt whole." No longer able to face Mike, she stared at the tea glass and the widening ring of dampness on the tablecloth beneath it.

Mike blew a low whistle. Gentle fingers lifted her chin to his gaze. "That night last fall, I thought you were a tigress and one tough babe. What you've overcome beats all that. You topped it with a college degree and a job helping families deal with kids in trouble like you were. A warrior. If I was wearing my uniform, I'd salute. No wonder Cleo is so loyal."

Andie could find nothing false in his voice or in his shining eyes or in his smile. Something thawed in her heart, and her chest seemed to expand with sweet warmth. Did he mean all that?

Chapter Five

NECK MUSCLES KNOTTED with tension, Mike waited for Andie's response. She was as unmoving as a marble statue except for her eyes. They peered at him with the same forensic intensity as her brother analyzing a case. What was she thinking?

The tentative way she'd begun and the breathless way she described her struggle must mean she expected rejection. Some asshole had rejected her. Made her feel like dirt. Made her doubt anyone would care. Likely why she was so reluctant to start something with him. Then for some reason, she'd opted to reveal her secrets. Had he passed or failed her test? Had he said too much?

He had secrets of his own. If she knew his family history, she'd understand why he saw what she'd achieved as so brave.

And then her gaze softened, morphing to relief and acceptance, and she squeezed his hand. She beamed him a wide smile, one of happiness and hope. It made him feel he'd stepped into a sunbeam. The knots in his neck untied, and he leaned closer to kiss that smile.

Lights started blinking out in the ballroom.

"Come on, you kids," one of the admirals barked as he passed them. Mike didn't know which, Hoot Chandler or Walter Devlin. "Party's over. Big day tomorrow."

Andie laughed and stood, still clutching his hand,

and they hit the door along with the others.

As they walked along the veranda, the soft night breeze washed away the tension, along with the fruity and sharp smells of the bar drinks. Mike longed to pull Andie close and reassure her, but they were surrounded by the few family members left awake at this late hour. Some aunts and uncles, the parents. No blonde whirlwind or Cleo's brothers, and Mike didn't see Lucas Del Rio and Mimi Ingram either. They must've crashed for the night while Andie was baring her soul. The two admirals, bickering loudly about who had more medals, led the pack.

Thomas Devlin, his fiancée on his left arm, walked five feet ahead of Mike and Andie. Much too close for him to whisper anything in her ear. Just his luck.

Around the corner beyond the ballroom, the lights were out. Shadows darkened, blending in with the night sky. As Devlin and Cleo passed porch furniture stacked against the wall, a crouched figure crept from cover.

The figure, a man, straightened and raised his right arm. A long blade glinted in the moonlight.

Adrenaline surged through Mike. He pushed Andie aside as he released the catch on his holster. "Stay back."

The man lunged at Devlin.

"Devlin, behind you!" Mike charged the attacker. Knocked him off balance.

Thomas Devlin pivoted and crouched, ready. Cleo stepped aside, off the veranda, pulling her mother with her. Women cried out and men shouted. DSF operatives rushed forward from the lawn's inky darkness.

"Give them room!" Devlin ordered.

Everyone stepped back in a ragged circle.

The attacker spun and jabbed the knife at Mike.

The move left the man open. Not a smooth recovery, and his hold wasn't best for hand-to-hand. Planting his feet, Mike grabbed the knife hand and pulled him closer. He hooked his left leg around the other man's right knee and yanked.

The man fell backward, as planned, taking Mike with him, not planned. Mike landed, hard, on his left shoulder. He grunted but held onto the knife hand. *Bastard.* He yanked upward and twisted.

The knife clattered onto the floor. Devlin kicked it out of reach.

Blocking the shooting pain in his shoulder, Mike twisted to his knees and shoved his 9mm under the attacker's chin. The twitchy guy. His sweat stank of fear.

"Now, scumbag, you have a good reason to twitch."

Andie's heart pounded in her ears. As the cold shivers on her spine began to subside, she allowed herself to exhale in a silent breath the scream trapped in her throat. Thomas was okay.

And Mike! Oh my God, Mike saved her brother's life.

Thomas drew Cleo into his arms, murmuring words Andie couldn't hear. Likely reassurances he was uninjured. His gaze found her too, and she nodded, giving him a thumbs-up. Tricky with quaking fingers.

Four operatives, including two women Andie hadn't spotted as such, surged past the old admirals, who'd hustled back toward the uproar. Brick and Hakim relieved Mike and hauled the attacker to his feet. The man offered no resistance, drooping in Brick's grasp as Hakim searched him.

"No weapons," Hakim said.

Mike pushed slowly to his feet and stowed his

smallish pistol beneath his sport coat. He rolled his left shoulder. Did the jerk stab him? He turned toward Andie and straightened. No blood visible, but the tight mouth and stiff posture meant he was in pain. She started toward him, but he held up a hand.

"Wait," he mouthed.

"Keep this man here," Thomas said. "Brick, you know this area. See if you can get the cops here silently. No need to wake everyone in the inn."

As Brick stepped away with his phone, another operative moved in to guard the prisoner, whose shoulders shook. Crying? Drunk? Or was something else going on?

Ah. Mike's jacket hid a holster. Were all these DSF people armed? Why didn't she realize this earlier? They were always armed. But here, at the wedding?

It had to be for more than gift protection. That was for damn sure. Keeping to the darkest shadows of the inn wall, she edged toward Mike.

"Nothing more to see here," Thomas said to the group. "This man had too much to drink and got scared when our crowd passed his napping place. Go to your rooms. I'll let you know if the police need statements."

Months ago, when Thomas and his people—Mike among them—had rescued her, Andie saw her brother in action. Even before that, she'd been the focus of his fiercely protective nature. And now these others witnessed his cool control and dynamic leadership. Pride lit their dad's face, and Cleo's dad clapped Thomas on the back.

"We'll make sure everyone's tucked in," Dad said, with a nod to his old friend.

Hoot Chandler agreed and looped arms with his

daughter and wife. The two admirals herded away the subdued partiers.

Everyone but Andie. Behind Mike, she wrapped her arms around his waist and took comfort in his scent, now tinged with the tang of sweat. She could feel the pistol, holstered just behind his right side, poking her, a reminder of the danger he'd faced.

"Ridiculous moves there. Thanks for saving my brother." She knew what his reply would be.

"Just doing my job." Exactly. An offhand acknowledgment. His voice was razor-edged with pain.

"You're hurt. Let me help."

"Pagano." Thomas crossed the floor and shook Mike's hand. "Quick thinking, man. Nice take-down. I owe you." He raised an eyebrow at Andie, plastered to Mike's back.

"Happened to be in the right place, sir. The others were too far away."

Andie's pulse kicked up again. Mike was right. If they hadn't been together, if he hadn't walked out with her, he wouldn't have been there to stop the attack. Even if she'd been behind Thomas, could she have warned him in time?

Her shoulders shook in an involuntary shudder. She manufactured a smile, a wobbly one, and moved around Mike. "Glad you're okay, bro."

"Right." His gaze went to his phone and then to Mike. "Cops just arrived. I'd appreciate it if you'd escort Andie to her room. Then report back here."

Heat rose to Andie's cheeks. "What is this, 1840? I can escort myself."

Crap. She thought she'd learned to control her knee-jerk reactions to Tommy's protectiveness. Now her impulsive reaction might've nixed her chance to be with Mike longer. And her opportunity to quiz him.

When she felt Thomas's hand on her shoulder, she didn't knock it away, like she used to when she'd fought his efforts to help her. She met his concerned gaze. "Sorry, I overreacted. But seriously, that guy's under guard. The danger's over. Or is it?"

His mouth curved in the indulgent smile people used for kittens and babies. She knew that smile. He wasn't going to level.

"Humor me." His strong arms drew her in for an embrace. "I've just been attacked. The big brass is escorting the other woman I love. Let me send in the Marine for you."

She hugged him back. "Love you, Tommy."

Releasing her, he turned to Mike. "I expect you back here in ten minutes, Pagano."

"Roger that, sir."

****

As Mike walked down the hall toward his room, he pulled his key from his pants pocket. Although electronic key cards would be more secure, the big brass key did fit the old inn's vibes.

If he hadn't been called to the slashed tires, it would've been to the drunk at the Devlin suite—guy on the wrong floor—or to the kitchen staff shooting at a flock of wild turkeys. The operatives who'd dealt with the shooting turned it over to hotel security. Those weren't diversions to pull DSF away, but he'd bet his gun the twitchy man and the slashed tires probably were.

He glanced at his phone. One a.m. If there were any more bad guys around, they better be snoring like he'd be in five minutes. He was wiped. He tried a cautious twist of his shoulder. A sharp jolt shot through the joint, and his breath caught. Ibuprofen and a hot shower ought to ease the sting.

He'd left Andie ticked off that she didn't know what was going on. She clearly didn't buy Devlin's spiel about the stabber being a drunk. He'd delivered her to her room, and by now she was probably asleep. Alone. Between the sheets. In some frilly thing or in nothing at all? His body tightened.

He gritted his teeth. If only the threat was over and he didn't have this subterfuge between them. But he didn't have to worry about squaring things with her until tomorrow. She was safe. Or was she? Hairs prickled on his nape, an instinctive warning that had saved his life more than once in Afghanistan.

He tapped the icon on his phone for the tracking app. When he spotted the green blip that was Andie's phone, alarm zipped up his spine. Not in her room. Not in any room on the second floor where all the family were staying.

Shit in a soup can! The blip located her on the fourth floor. He looked up and down the hall, then at his door.

Here.

He used his key and opened the door.

"Don't shoot, Marine."

His breath whooshed out as he entered the room. Andie uncrossed her legs and climbed off the bed—his bed, his king-size bed. The words on her tee, stretched across her full breasts, read, "It takes one to know one."

Automatically setting the security lock, he dragged his gaze away from her jutting nipples, but only to stare at the way the tight knit pants outlined her body. His sister wore the same kind of pants, but never looked like this. As good as his fantasy. No, better. She was here, live, and her eyes had the welcoming glow of candlelight. Her smile hit him with incendiary force. A wave of anticipation rushed through his blood.

Twisting to toss the key on the desk earned him another stab in the damn shoulder.

"Don't be angry." Unease darkened the sparkle in her gaze, and she stopped moving toward him. Knitted her fingers together.

"Not mad." He sucked in a breath, determined not to let the pain take hold, as he attempted to transform his grimace into a grin. "Just, how'd you get in?"

"With my official DSF lock-pick, of course." She propped a hand on her hip and grinned.

He scraped a hand through his hair. "Andie—"

"Never mind that. You're injured, and I brought medical supplies. Um, well, depending on what you need. There, on the desk."

He hadn't even noticed, had seen only her. Beside his keys were a heating pad, a bottle of some kind of lotion, bandages, and antiseptic.

The teasing smile left her eyes, replaced by warmth and gentleness, as she stepped closer. "Where did that creep hurt you?"

"He didn't hurt me. I mean, it's my shoulder. Got dislocated a couple years ago. It hurts once in a while, especially when I take a whack, like tonight when I landed on it. A little heat—" he eyed the heating pad "—and a couple pain killers, and I'll be fine."

He kept talking for no reason, blathering stupid excuses, which didn't deter her from moving in on him, close enough that the scent of her hair and the hint of musk that was the natural essence of her skin drew him toward her.

"Uh huh." Her warm hands smoothed up his chest and slid the jacket off his shoulders and down his arms. She draped it on the desk chair and went to work on his belt buckle. Her slender fingers glided beneath his waistband, sparking tingles in their wake as his shirt came free. "Love this sexy silk tee. Oh, and you'll want to lose that gun and holster too."

Her low voice, syrup thick, mesmerized him, heated him like a steam bath. In spite of his exhaustion, lust shot through him. He swelled and hardened instantaneously. What was it about this woman that no matter how tired—or hurt—he was, his reaction to her was intense?

When she flitted away to the bathroom, he blinked away her spell. "What are you doing?"

She returned with one of the inn's thick white towels. "Remember, I'm here to make you feel better. What you need is a massage and heat."

Heat he already had, in spades. But she probably meant the electric kind. A massage. Reality clicked in, reinforced when she picked up the lotion. She hadn't come for sex, not that he was in any shape for sex, except for the part of him that was sitting up and begging for it.

"Yeah, a massage would be perfect." He crossed to the bed, where he withdrew the 9mm and set it on the bedside stand. The holster and belt came off next. The tee required some maneuvering, but he managed with her help. While he stowed the pistol, extra magazine, and holster in the bedside drawer, she pulled down the blanket and sheets, then spread out the oversize towel.

He shed his shoes and stretched out on his belly, taking care with his left arm as he placed his hands beside his shoulders. "I don't get how you managed all this, but thanks."

The mattress gave a little as she knelt beside him and then straddled his hips. Her sweet little ass pressed into his butt, and every cell in his body sprang to attention.

Her husky laugh vibrated into his back, making him clench his fists. "The spa's people are doing the bridal party's hair and makeup tomorrow, so when I told the manager one of our group was injured, she was eager to supply whatever I wanted. She gave me lotion with ylang-ylang for muscle tension and geranium for relaxation." She sniffed. "Green plants, roses—that's the ylang-ylang. I smell lavender too."

And then her hands were on his back and both shoulders, smoothing the massage lotion. Roses or geranium, he didn't care, but sexy for damn sure. Heavenly torture having her hands slipping and sliding on his bare skin. Having his massive hard-on mashed into the mattress provided camouflage. Nothing he could do but bear up and enjoy.

He drifted, in free fall, as she kneaded with fingers stronger than he'd expected and the heels of her hands. After a while, her hypnotizing ministrations eased into gentler rubs and caresses.

"While I waited for you, I had a long time to think."

Her sultry voice came from just behind his ear. The light pressure of her breasts snuggled against his back. "Mmm, that's good," he murmured.

"Especially about some of the odd things that happened today. One, I counted at least seven DSF operatives in and around the inn. All armed, including you, with your inside-the-waistband holster. Overkill for wedding-gift protection, I'd say. And concealed, even from me. Or should I say, *especially* from me?"

Mike came instantly alert, and his eyes flew open. The only response he could think of was a repeat. "Mr. Security, remember?" He raised his head and started to turn over, but her amazingly strong thighs clamped his waist, and her hands pressed on his shoulders. He stayed put, suspecting where this interrogation was headed.

She huffed in reply. "Two, no way Thomas would leave the yacht unlocked. Even if he did, he'd never send an operative. For something personal, he'd go himself. And three, I don't believe for a second that the man who attacked him was only a drunk. So, Mike, what the hell is really going on?"

Her weight left him as she slid over and sat beside him on the bed.

He pushed up, surprised to find the movement caused minimal discomfort. Despite her motive, her kneading had eased the pain, likely the inflammation too. He turned over, stacked up pillows, and leaned back. "Thanks for the great massage. Where'd you learn to do that?"

Sitting cross-legged, she shook her head. "Don't make me repeat my question."

Dammit, she must've learned interrogation from Devlin. Or it was in the family DNA. He swallowed, adjusted his position. "The boss wanted everything kept quiet so the inn personnel, members of the wedding, and guests weren't upset."

"Too late. This member of the wedding is already upset." She pursed her mouth. "You can probably count Cleo among the upset and suspicious. I'm sure she's grilling Thomas right now. So give."

And the boss would cave, so he couldn't fault Mike for doing the same. "DSF has been chasing the players in a major art theft ring. I'm one of the operatives on the case, made more urgent since the gang robbed a big museum in Baltimore two months ago."

"The Centre Street Museum. They got away with millions in paintings, cut from their frames. They killed two security guards, and no one can identify any gang members. I know all that. Y'all were yakking about it last month at Mara and Cort's barbecue."

Of course she knew, but it surprised him she remembered. He plowed on. "Recent intel said we were close, but the gang planned an attack to stop us, specifically this weekend. It was too late to move the wedding somewhere more secure. At this inn, where people come and go unchecked, it's next to impossible to vet everyone and keep track."

"Aha. The reason for so many company personnel." A frown pleated her forehead. "That man who jumped Thomas? Piss-poor planning for such a sophisticated gang."

"Yeah, he's no pro. Sure didn't know how to fight with or without a knife. My old high-school wrestling move took him down easy. The Anne Arundel County police say he refuses to say anything. We're waiting for information on his identity. Maybe we'll catch a break linking him to the gang. But it's likely that wasn't the main event." Also likely that the boss would ream out somebody for missing twitchy guy's ambush spot on the veranda.

It wasn't lost on him that he was omitting his role in her protection. His chest tightened, like his sternum had taken a hit. If he confessed now, no telling how she'd react. No, he knew exactly how. Didn't she tell him earlier how much she'd hated her brother's high-handed protectiveness? She might not let Mike near her the rest of the weekend, leaving her a sitting duck in a satin dress. He couldn't risk it. He had to protect her. He'd tell her after it was all over. She'd understand.

Sure she would.

"But you don't have a clue what they're really planning?" Fear deepened in her eyes.

He straightened, relieved not to feel pangs in his shoulder. He leaned forward, placed a hand on her knee. "We're looking into all possibilities. Don't panic. We have this covered."

"Okay then." She picked up her phone from beside her on the bed. "I'll be another pair of eyes and ears for shady characters or anything strange. What's your cell number?"

His blood pressure shot for the moon. Oh man, the last thing the team needed was a determined amateur sleuth putting herself in the middle of things. She was so focused on making sure the wedding went off perfectly that she'd endanger herself. Now he was sweating for a reason that had nothing to do with their chemistry. Shit, how could he stop her? "You know, telling you all this means I've broken protocol."

"Not really. I'd figured out most of it, just not who might be behind it. And I'll keep it to myself."

"Good. Perfect, and not just for that reason, but Mr. D doesn't want everyone on edge." He recited his number for her. "Put it on speed dial. Call me for anything that seems off. And, Andie, don't play detective."

"I don't like this secrecy, but I'll have to trust Thomas. And you." Her smile was back—not the brilliant one, but a sultry one. The heat that shimmered between them made him light-headed, or maybe it was the fact that his blood supply had taken a detour south.

Her tongue peeked out and licked her lips. "So if there's still danger, maybe I shouldn't go all the way downstairs and sleep in my room. Alone."

Oh man, if she was taking this big step with him, he'd damned well make sure he showed her he cared, make sure he deserved her trust. He should take her back to her room, but she'd see it as rejection.

And reject her, he couldn't.

He gathered her in his arms. "If you stay with me, I'll keep you safe, but neither of us will get much sleep."

Chapter Six

RELIEF SIGHED THROUGH Andie as Mike pulled her against his chest. His mouth cruised over hers, and then he deepened the kiss. Her body throbbed with each graze of his tongue. Long, deep thrills made her want to climb into his skin.

Seduction wasn't her thing, but tonight, the undeniable heat of mutual desire had made her bold. He was romantic and tender, funny and charming, physical and sexy as hell.

She pressed her palms against his chest, and her insides went all shivery and hot. He was only a few inches taller than her, but tough and capable. She'd known he was buff, but yowza, seeing him with his shirt off shot sparks through her nerve endings. A wrestler's trim body, all honed muscularity in his shoulders and arms—*Semper Fi* tat on his right bicep —a sleek and compact torso. Massaging his firm flesh tangled all her circuits, and now she had her hands on his impressive pecs.

"Andie," he breathed into her mouth.

"Nice." She threaded her fingers through his dark chest hairs. "Soft, and not too much."

His face was flushed and his gray eyes dark as charcoal. He frowned. "Soft? I'm so hard I can barely breathe."

She licked one flat, copper-colored nipple, making him twitch. "I was referring to your body hair."

As his mouth found hers again, his rumbling chuckle flashed tingles through her. Her entire body throbbed, and she wrapped her arms around him, tracing the deep indent of his spine with her fingers. His left hand pushed beneath her tee and caressed her ribs, her stomach, the rasp of his callused fingers setting off new flames. One finger, then a second, teased a nipple through her silk bra.

"Now you're the one wearing too many clothes." He grasped the tee and yanked it upward and off. "I have to know. Strawberry or cherry."

"Now who's sounding cryptic?"

His right hand flicked the clasp of her bra, and he tossed it away. His gaze fixed on her nipples. "Ah, strawberry pink, my favorite." He tugged her down to lie beside him and drew his hand slowly over her breasts, cupping the curves, and gliding a fingertip across them. He tongued his way down her throat to her tight nipples. Heat spiraled from her breasts through her whole body. "You are so beautiful."

"My turn." She licked his shoulder, his chest, absorbing his salty taste, then stroked his taut belly. She didn't fight the urge to delve deeper, but the waistband fastening defeated her. "Pants." She shed her yoga pants and panties in a flash and lay back.

Suddenly her throat felt thick and tight. She had no qualms about him seeing her in the buff. She kept herself strong and fit, but did he still wonder about her? "Um, Mike, I want you to know that when I was messed up and on the street, I stayed clean. No diseases. I'm sorry about all I did, but I never—"

He cut her off with a hard kiss. "Never apologize to me again for what lost and angry teenage Andie did or didn't do. Sometime I'll tell you about my family. Okay?" The gray of his eyes was steel, reinforcing his demand.

Tenderness welled up at his softly uttered words, in contrast to his fierce kiss. She cupped his bristly jaw. "Okay."

His hands fumbled with the zipper, but finally he shucked his pants and, she noted, green boxer briefs. His arousal sprang free, as impressive as she'd anticipated.

And then he was kissing her again, holding her tight against his naked body, and she reveled in the roughness of his skin against hers, of the tang of sweat mingling with the massage lotion, of the hot ridge pressing against her stomach. His fingers found her moist heat with unerring aim and rubbed, stirring insistent pulsations inside her. She wrapped her hand around his shaft and squeezed and stroked. He jerked in her hand.

"I want you. Now!" As if he couldn't tell.

"Protection. In the drawer." He rolled away from her. Foil crackled. Sheathed, he turned to her, covering her body with his and probing between her thighs. His heat burned her skin, and her heart raced. He filled her vision, all dark eyed and rugged, passion rolling off him in waves. A moan or a growl slipped from his throat.

"Your shoulder."

"All better, and my other pain's about to be cured." His voice, low and savage with need, made her thigh muscles quiver.

When he slid inside her, a raw jolt of sensation shot to the pit of her stomach, and she stiffened and gasped.

"You okay?"

"Absolutely. Just, it's been a while and… don't stop."

His kisses brushed her eyes, her nose, as if he was giving her time to adjust. But she needed no time, needed only him. She grasped his head and kissed him with all the pent-up desire scorching her.

On a growl, he began to move. He was huge and hard, and all she could do was hold onto his shoulders and wrap her legs around his waist and hang on. His breath was harsh and hot against her ear. He filled her again and again, deeper, moving and stroking over and over, melting her insides. This man, this one man, was making her feel an exhilaration, an intensity she'd never experienced before. Then all cognitive ability vacated the premises and she could only feel as she rode rising waves of sensation, and then shock waves rolled through her with the force of a summer storm and she cried out at the swamping, spangling undulations. Above her, his body stiffened and he drove into her one last time as he shuddered with the force of his release.

He collapsed on top of her, his heart thumping in time with hers. He kissed her and rolled aside, pulled up the covers, and tucked her against his right side. "What *was* that, a runaway freight train?"

Smiling, she pressed a kiss to his shoulder and slanted her leg across his. "Runaway something. I think you call it sex, or chemistry, or both."

"Give me a little while, and we can see if that chemical reaction can be replicated."

"You're on."

"You promised to answer my questions."

"I promised nothing. What questions?"

"How you got into the room, and forget the lock pick

routine. And where you learned how to give a massage."

"Oh, *those* questions. The desk clerk bought the same story as the spa lady and gave me your room number. All I had to do was show the maid the first-aid supplies, and she let me in. As for the massage skills, I worked at a spa for a couple years. One of the massage therapists gave me some tips. No biggie."

"Pretexting like a P.I."

"What texting?"

"Pretexting. It means lying to obtain privileged information."

"Oh, like a P.I., I get it." She huffed, inordinately pleased. "In my psych classes, the same thing was called social engineering to manipulate people. My pretexting was more along the line of white lies."

"So you could get into my room." He hugged her closer. "Don't let this go to your head, but you've found security holes that inn management will need to fix pronto. You're a dangerous woman, Andie Devlin." His smiling lips grazed her mouth, giving the lie to his words.

The bedside light went off, and in less than thirty seconds, his breathing slowed and evened out. Asleep and still embracing her.

Andie snuggled against him, holding to her the heady aftermath of their loving—and it *was* lovemaking, not simply sex to satisfy an itch. Mike made her feel more than desire, something ineffable that took her breath away, that made her feel good about herself. That she wasn't damaged goods. He seemed to *get* her, even her regrettable past, and that she'd overcome it. He'd said he wanted more than this weekend, and tonight created a connection with him she ached to explore. So maybe she'd take the plunge, and if it all fell apart, at least she'd have this memory. Closing her eyes, she let herself drift into sleep.

She was dreaming of hot kisses on her neck and breasts, of sensation between her legs.

"Andie." Mike's deep voice was in her ear. Or was it only the rumble of the air-conditioner?

She blinked, waking, her head muzzy with sleep, to find his naked body tight against her beneath the covers.

"You up for that chemistry experiment?"

Awareness clicked in, and she turned over to kiss him, enveloped in his heat and the wild taste of his mouth and the part of him that was definitely up and throbbing against her belly. "I am. Got another test tube?"

"The gift shop sells 'em by the dozen."

"You didn't."

"Start counting."

Then he proceeded to demonstrate that the craving between them went way beyond chemistry. They made love more slowly, savoring every lush, lazy stroke, every languid kiss before driving to a final burst of wrenching, drenching release.

****

In the morning, after delivering Andie to her room, Mike hustled back upstairs to shower and shave. He donned a clean tee, jeans, and the black sport coat.

Finding that he had a good range of motion without pain, he grinned. A massage followed by spectacular sex was obviously the cure. Reliving her responsiveness, her trust, and her sweet passion spread heat through his body and light into the dark corner of his soul, where he'd relegated his grief. She'd come to him, for healing and, yes, answers, but also because she wanted him despite fearing rejection. She was brave and tough and smart, and he wanted her all over again.

He paused while settling the pistol in its holster. It seemed they both were disregarding his working for her brother as a reason to avoid involvement. Hell, if Devlin confronted him about it, he'd deal.

Andie was having breakfast with Cleo in the dining room and had promised not to leave the inn without him. In the afternoon, she'd be safe enough in the spa with the other female members of the wedding party, doing their hair and God knew what else in preparation for the wedding.

Satisfied the gun lay flat, well concealed beneath his jacket, he headed down the hall to Brick's room. He moved aside room-service trays and knocked.

"Yo, Romeo." A grinning Brick admitted him, and then crossed the room to the desk and took a seat at a laptop.

Maybe he—and possibly more of the others—knew or guessed about Andie and him, but Mike saw no point in responding to the jibe and verifying anything.

The team leader's suite was equipped with two more laptops set up on a folding table as well as the one on the desk. The open bedroom door revealed an unmade bed, the covers folded back neatly. Stark contrast to Mike's rumpled bed. If they used standard protocol for a hotel-room command post, Brick or another operative would stand guard while a maid—usually a nervous maid—serviced the room. A neat bed expedited that process.

"Any more intel on last night's knifer?" Mike made a beeline to the bagels and coffee set up on the bureau. Caffeine and an everything bagel in hand, he dropped into the armchair beside the desk.

Brick's thick fingers tapped keys. "Maryland

license in his wallet IDs him as Norman Torres, age forty-five, address in Dundalk, a suburb of Baltimore. A few negligible traffic violations, but no criminal record. Not registered at the inn, but the key fob in his pocket located his car in the lot. Older sedan. Bills and repair receipts inside, same I.D.. The county detective in charge told me this morning Torres is out of work, and a stroke confined his wife to a wheelchair. When he called, she was frantic with worry why her Norman wasn't home."

"She have any idea why her husband would try to knife a stranger here? Or was he a stranger? The boss didn't recognize the man, but maybe he knew Devlin or the company?"

Brick shook his head. "She claimed she'd never heard of Thomas Devlin or DSF or the Riverside Inn. The detective's going to talk to her more today." A ping sounded from the computer. "Hold on. Maybe there's more."

Mike chewed on his bagel. There had to be some connection to the art theft gang. Nothing else made sense. Unlikely some other lowlife wanted Devlin dead. Too coincidental. But how did Torres, who didn't have an obvious link to crime, get mixed up in this?

When Brick looked his way, Mike said, "Torres is hard up. What if somebody paid him to stab Devlin?"

"Give the man a kewpie doll." The stocky man jerked a nod at the laptop screen. "That was the county detective. Money was deposited this morning in the Torres family account. Wire transfer from an untraceable account in the Caymans. Twenty-five grand."

The Caymans. Big money was behind this. Mike emitted a low whistle. "It has to be the Centre Street Museum thieves. The assholes are scared we're closing in. When I first spotted Torres, he was acting jumpy. In my head, I called him *twitchy guy*. He was drinking to bolster his courage but had to wait for a chance at Devlin. So why choose this guy as hit man? And how'd they find him? He's no career criminal, just a guy down on his luck."

"And inept. The knife came from the inn kitchen. One of the sous chefs admitted leaving it on a platter in the bar."

"A weapon of opportunity." Mike thought that over. "Like he didn't plan on the attack? What's he say?"

"So far, zip. Just rocks back and forth in his cell or has his head in his hands. Hasn't called his wife or anybody else. Eventually we'll find a connection. Brick rolled the chair back and linked his hands behind his head. "Again, why hire a mope like him, not a professional, to carry out some sort of attack on Devlin or the wedding?"

"Like we said about the tire vandalism, maybe it's a distraction from what they're really plotting. Or Torres was a decoy, meant to pull our guys away from their posts."

"Lot of money to pay a decoy. After the excitement was over, a general search of the inn and grounds found nothing suspicious. So we still have no idea what they're plotting or who might be involved. We need all our eyes and ears on this one." Brick slammed a wide palm on the desk.

Mike's nerves tingled. *Andie.* She'd used the same phrase, *eyes and ears*. And dammit, she never promised *not* to play detective. His gut knotted with a vicious twist.

"Think I'll go through the background checks. Maybe something will pop." He crossed to one of the other laptops and opened to the research reports. Head of research, Mara Marton Jones, had her people working overtime on this. They'd come up with info on dozens of employees and guests in a short time. But Mara and her husband would be attending the wedding, so her staff would be on their own. He wanted this over before that.

An hour later, a second bagel and two more mugs of coffee firing his nerves, he had nothing concrete, only gut suspicions about employees recently hired for the summer rush. Maybe he ought to go have a chat with one or two while he had time.

Chapter Seven

SURROUNDED BY THE swish of satin and the
fragrance of roses and sweet peas, Andie smoothed her
knee-length dress. In a few hours, the wedding and
reception would be over, with only minor disasters, all
averted. Then she could breathe again.

Beside her, Cleo's mom helped her daughter
wriggle into her strapless white gown. Across the living
room of the senior Chandlers' suite, co-opted as their
dressing room, Trudy pinned stray strands into Mimi's
curly chignon. And Felicity? In the bathroom or
bedroom, doing who knew what. She seemed to be
fussing to herself.

Andie checked herself in the floor-length mirror.
Her hair wasn't long enough for the curly chignon, but
the hairdresser had pinned it back in a small cascade of
curls and perfectly matched the coral streak in her hair to
the bodice's shade.

Falling from the waist, the satin skirt swirled with
gorgeous hues of coral, salmon, mauve and other shades
Andie couldn't name. Cleo had designed the fabric,
copying the dawn sky from one of her paintings.

The dress was so fantastic Andie was terrified she'd
drop cake or something worse on it and ruin the only
painting of Cleo's she could ever afford to own.

What would Mike think when he saw her?

Remembering last night heated her inside and out, and she pressed a palm to her stomach. He'd told her the truth about why DSF staff were skulking around. And then he'd been hungry for her and sweet and romantic, and he made her feel all soft inside and want more than she'd thought she could have.

"What are you grinning at?" Cleo asked.

Oops, grinning like a fool at nothing. Well, not nothing. "You. You're amazing, and in a little while you'll be more than my best friend. You'll be my sister."

Irene was lacing up the back of the ivory gown. Cleo was beyond pretty, and in that gown, simply stunning. Below the embroidered bodice, the long satin skirt flared slightly and had a short train, temporarily buttoned up and out of the way. She looked radiant and so happy that Andie's heart swelled with love and admiration.

"Me? You're the amazing one."

Blinking back tears, Irene placed a hand on each of their shoulders. "You two are going to make me cry even before the ceremony. Andie, I've thought of you as a second daughter for years. I'm beyond ecstatic our families will be joined."

Tears stung Andie's eyes. She kissed the older woman's cheek. "Thanks, Mom Irene. Me too. But no messing up the mascara."

"How much time, Andie?" Cleo asked.

"Ten minutes. Give me a sec, and I'll go see if the men are ready." She also wanted to try phoning her roommate one more time before she had to give up her evening purse to Trudy, who was the Guardian of Everything, including keeping everyone on schedule.

She left them checking the bridal bouquet, white and coral roses and tiny trailing daisies, and walked across the living room to Mimi and her mom, who'd caught her eye in the mirror and beckoned to her. "Problem?"

Mimi whispered, "Felicity, eh? She's trying to get the spa hairdresser to come here and do some major fix on her hair."

"What's wrong with her hair?"

"Nothing." Trudy's lips twitched. "We don't have time for this, but she won't listen to me."

Andie huffed. Super Maid of Honor to the rescue. Cheerful smile pasted on, she marched through the bedroom and to the open bathroom door. Hit by Felicity's magnolia cloud, she backed up a step. "What's up, y'all?"

In front of the bathroom mirror, Cleo's sister-in-law set down her phone. "This hairstyle simply won't do, and the hairdresser says she can take me in fifteen minutes." She poked the tail of a rat-tail comb into the curly chignon, similar to Mimi's and Cleo's, except for the floral coronet decorating Cleo's. "A smoother, tighter style suits me better."

Felicity's meddling had crammed the schedule with massages and a girls' luncheon, leaving no time for anything extra. A slow boil bubbled in Andie's chest, and she tamped it down with a deep breath. Berating the woman for her interference or railing about her self-centered bitchiness wasn't the way to go.

"I simply have to disagree," Andie cooed in a honey-chile accent. "Your blonde hair shines like the sun, and the loops and ringlets are so contemporary and youthful. Everyone will think you're the same age as Cleo." Who was at least twelve years younger. Andie crossed mental fingers. And toes.

Felicity's eyes widened, and she turned back to the

mirror. Tilted her head one way, then the other. "You really think so?"

After Andie choked out a few more compliments, a mollified Felicity picked up her nosegay of white rose and coral peonies and joined the others, ready to proceed. Another disaster averted. *Let it be the final one, and now everything will be perfect.*

****

Andie whisked to the ballroom, to a spot where she ought to be able to see whether Thomas, Lucas, and Cleo's brothers stood in their places in the wedding tent. Dangling from her arm, her metallic evening bag banged against her side. The thing weighed a ton, but it matched the evening's color scheme and was big enough for her phone.

Hydrangea and coral peony centerpieces decorated the tables, along with the favors, stoneware coasters decorated by the bride. She headed past the bar.

Dressed for the formal evening in a white shirt and black vest, Steve was stowing glassware behind the bar. "Hey, Andie, looking hot."

She sent him a quick smile. "Thanks." She halted at the open doorway when she saw Thomas and Mike on the veranda, deep in discussion.

"Nothing then," Thomas said.

"Guests all accounted for," Mike replied. "A few people eyed Brick when he was hovering behind Cleo's friends who were checking names and handing out programs, but nobody struck him as suspicious or headed for the hills. We're nearly home free, sir."

The two men hadn't noticed her, so she could take time to drink in the sight of Mike in a black suit, white shirt, vest, and a tie. Pleasure welled up, carrying with it the flush of heat.

Thomas shook Mike's hand. "Thanks for keeping my sister safe. I knew what I was doing when I assigned you to protect her this weekend."

Her brother's words rooted her high heels to the floor. The rest of what he said was drowned out by white noise in her ears. Her heart beat with hard thumps that hurt her chest. When she heard herself whimper, she gritted her teeth.

She'd known deep down, hadn't she, that Mike being with her for real was too good to be true?

He turned, his gaze finding her. The tightening of his mouth and the sharpened awareness in his eyes told her he knew she'd heard Thomas's damning praise.

She forced her chin up and her feet forward, one leaden step at a time. Her heels cracked like gunshots on the veranda's wood floor. She looked only at her brother, her *oblivious* brother, not at Mike, who'd stepped aside.

Thomas turned, an anxious look on his face. "Hey, kid, you look terrific. What's taking so long in there? My calls to Cleo went to voice mail."

She managed a small, tight smile and hoped he would think her merely nervous, as he clearly was. "Phones are turned off and stashed away. Except mine. But we're ready. Cleo sent me to see if you were."

"Let's do this. Can't wait to get my bride on the *Prowler* and safely away from, um, away." Still unaware of the tension radiating between Mike and her, he kissed her on the forehead and strode away toward the wedding tent.

His face as red as if he'd just bit into a jalapeño, Mike reached for her arm, but she twisted away. "Andie, it's not what you think."

"It's exactly what I think. You led me to believe you were with me because you wanted to be, because you wanted me. When I bared my soul to you, you swore that didn't bother you."

"It didn't. And everything I said was true. *Is* true. Devlin put me in the middle of this. It had to be confidential. I was going—"

It was all she could do not to fly at his lying face with both fists. "Bullshit! You told me about the art theft plot, didn't you? So you could've explained that I was your assignment— *before* you made love to me. Yes, after I knew you weren't seriously injured, I threw myself at you, but because I believed what was between us was real, not the sham it obviously is. You're despicable and a damn liar."

"I never meant to hurt you. I do want to be with you. The protection gig complicates everything." His shoulders heaved, and he blew out a breath.

"Well, allow me to fix that little problem. Go ahead and do your damn job. Protect me, but keep your distance."

Knees threatening to give way, she turned and walked back into the ballroom. She sank onto a chair at the first table she came to and gripped the edge of the table so hard her fingers hurt. Thank God the bartender had vanished, and no one was here to see her fall apart. She fought the urge to howl and let the tears come. She couldn't give in. Not yet.

She owed Thomas and Cleo their perfect wedding.

Muffled buzzing came from her evening purse, which dangled from her wrist like an alien device. With stiff fingers, she pulled out her phone. Trudy. She cleared her throat.

"Andie? Cleo wants to know if Thomas has left on the honeymoon yacht without her." With laughter in the background, the woman's words rang with humor.

Head high, Andie schooled her voice into Super Maid of Honor mode. "Not a chance. Tell the beautiful bride her handsome groom awaits."

Chapter Eight

MIKE FLEXED HIS fingers and stood at parade rest as he waited at the back of the wedding tent. Down front to one side of the Navy chaplain, stood Thomas Devlin, then Lucas Del Rio and Cleo's two brothers, all looking as tense as he felt. As the processional music began, something measured and romantic, played by last night's duo plus a violinist, Mike fastened open the tent flap.

First Mimi Ingram, then the blonde whirlwind ironically named Felicity. Smiling, they joined the tuxedoed men waiting by the chaplain, who peered down the aisle over his glasses.

Next would come the maid of honor.

Mike's gut tightened. Head held high and a stiff smile on her lips, Andie entered. As she passed him, she stumbled on the uneven grass. He reached for her elbow to steady her, but she shook him off. Despite the warm evening, he could swear he felt the chill coming off her.

And no wonder. He'd screwed up big time by not telling her everything last night. She'd have been pissed off, but he could've talked her off the ledge. The shock in her eyes at Devlin's disclosure nearly cracked Mike's chest. Even now a two-ton land mine crowded against his sternum. He hurt her badly. She believed he lied to her about everything. He deserved all the things she accused him of, and he had to find a way to talk to her. Maybe later she'd cool down and listen? Not likely.

He still had a job to do—watching the crowd, along with Brick and two others—and protecting Andie. Before he lost it and ran cursing across the lawn, he dug deep for the calm he'd learned in the Marines, controlling his breathing until his emotions settled.

Andie made her way to her place beside the others and nodded to the musicians, who changed the tune to something classical he sort of recognized. Everyone turned toward the back.

As Cleo, on her father's arm, stepped forward, Mike could practically feel the beams from her glowing face.

"Wait, wait!" Trudy Ingram hunkered down behind her. "The train, eh, sweetie?"

Cleo pulled up and smiled at the glitch. No nerves on her part, but Admiral Chandler's Adam's apple jumped a couple of times.

"You know," she said, "Andie would've noticed this little problem if she wasn't distracted by something—or someone. I wonder what that's about." She sent him a knowing wink.

He swallowed and managed a *no idea* shrug.

Thankfully, the hem pulled free from whatever had bound it, and she continued forward.

Trudy scooted past him and took her seat in the back row. Max Rivera, beside his wife Kate, had been assigned to save it for her. He jerked a nod Mike's way. A pat on his suit coat at the four o'clock position indicated his holster. Max was ready if needed.

Mike nodded in response. He'd attended their wedding in December, and Max had proudly announced last week they were expecting their first child. On Kate's other side, Mara turned and gave him that little curly wave women did. No big wedding for her and Cort, only a small gathering in April at their house in Virginia. Devlin and Cleo went, but the Centre Street Museum heist had pulled Mike out of town. He spotted a few other DSF staff scatted among the guests.

Cleo arrived at Devlin's side and the ceremony began. She was a beautiful bride. Hell, weren't they all?

But Andie in that pink and, um, pink*ish* dress, with her hair held back in curls his fingers itched to touch, blew him away. Like earlier. Probably why he tripped over his tongue when she was flailing his skin down to blood and bone. He couldn't regret making love with her. Not one moment of it—her sleek curves and sweet flesh, his body aflame as she wrapped her hand around him, her sighs as they moved in sync, the wild exhilaration between them and the intimacy afterward.

She held her head high, going through the rehearsed motions. Pale as porcelain, her expression looked flash-frozen.

They'd barely found the way to each other. He had to make this right.

Applause and music with a brisk beat—"Signed, Sealed, Delivered"—snapped him out of his funk. The bride and groom were kissing, so the Navy chaplain must've just pronounced them husband and wife.

On Brick's cue, Mike joined him where the receiving line would stand. None of the guests seemed out of place, but now they'd be in hand-shaking and cheek-kissing—or attacking—distance. Somebody could be carrying, so they had to be ready. Mike and Brick took up positions behind Devlin and his bride. Two other operatives stood farther along the line.

The wedding party walked out, pair by pair, Andie on Lucas Del Rio's arm. The big operative slanted Mike a questioning look as Andie swept by without looking his way.

****

As the last of the wedding cake was served, a drum roll hushed the crowd. The combo was now larger by three instruments and a vocalist, who acted as emcee. She announced the couple, and Thomas and Cleo stepped hand-in-hand onto the dance floor.

Andie's throat clogged with tears. Although she'd taken a kick in the teeth today, now was the time to concentrate on happiness for these two people she fiercely loved. Leaving Lucas, Mimi Ingram edged around the throng and hugged her.

"I saw Cleo's randy uncle coming your way. Thought I'd head him off."

Sure enough, the man who'd been hitting on Andie had turned aside. She slipped an arm around her new semi-cousin's waist. "You're the best."

The vocalist launched into the classic "At Last," and the combo increased the tempo to a danceable beat. The crowd hushed, rapt, as Thomas swung Cleo into his arms.

Their waltz featured twirls and lifts and side-by-side quick steps. *My brother can dance?* Well, not exactly. He was a little stiff, but obviously the sneaky pair had taken ballroom dancing lessons. When the song ended, a deep dip and a long kiss (with tongues!) earned wild applause, stomping, and wolf whistles.

Andie and Mimi jumped up and down, clapping.

When the ovation subsided, Andie's palms stung. When the next song began, pinging nerves tempered her joy.

The vocalist tapped the microphone. "Please give it up for the bride's parents, Admiral and Mrs. Horace Chandler, and for the groom's father and sister, Admiral Walter Devlin and Ms. Andrea Devlin."

To polite clapping, Hoot and Irene began dancing to "Can You Feel the Love Tonight?" Andie's father crossed the floor, holding out his hand to her. Almost as tall as Thomas, he was lean and fit, his hair still thick, but now silver. Judging from her cramping jaw, her expression probably mirrored his rigid one.

With a mix of trepidation and regret, she accepted that warm, strong hand, the hand that hadn't held hers since her mother died. Maybe teenage anger and rebellion blocked out good memories, the few, the far between. Looking past his shoulder at nothing, she followed his lead in a simple box step.

They'd lost their way, and she had no idea how to scale the wall between them. They danced without speaking until her chest grew so tight she thought it might explode. She looked up at his lined face and blurted out, "It should be Mom you're dancing with."

His gaze met hers, and his jaw worked. "The same thought crossed my mind, but I'm glad it's you in her place. You look like her, you know."

The tune changed to "Endless Love," and other couples swept onto the dance floor. Andie's throat tightened. Were they supposed to sit down now? She couldn't remember. Now that they were talking, sort of, she didn't want their dance to end.

To her amazement, he kept her in his arms. She moved with him in whatever this dance of theirs was. "Thanks, Dad. I —"

"I'm good as long as they keep playing something slow." He smiled, a sheepish little-boy grin that was gone so quickly she might've imagined it. "I have some things to say, and if we stop dancing, I might not get out the words." He cleared his throat. "It's been a long time since I was a good father. Hell, I was probably never much of a father, but after Wendy died, I failed you and Tommy."

"It was a rough time for us all." She swallowed hard, but the swollen knot in her throat refused to dissolve. Guilting him *now* for all of what happened then and her long road back seemed wrong. "And then I made it harder."

His eyebrows slapped together in a hard expression. "Don't. Yes, you went off the deep end, but I let it happen without knowing why or how to help you." He drew a deep breath. "A friend has helped me understand that better recently. How about this? No more blame game. We start over, from here."

Tears burned her eyes. "A new start. Yes."

He released her hand and hugged her tight. "You're my daughter, Andrea Faye Devlin. I love you. I never stopped."

She let the tears fall on the starched crispness of his shirt. "I love you too, Dad."

Another set of arms came around them. When she looked up, it was into Thomas's glittering gaze.

"At last," her brother said, his voice liquid with emotion. "Now we can be a family again."

She hugged him back and started to walk off the dance floor because the band had sped up the tempo by a mile. Neither man would be eager to stick around for "Old Time Rock and Roll."

"Don't go. I have more to tell you." A rush of pink colored her dad's cheeks as he led Thomas and her aside.

****

An hour later, Andie was ready to sit out the next song, but Mimi and two of Cleo's college friends dragged her back for one more line dance. *Oh, great.* Why did it have to be "Hurt So Good"? Freaking perfect. And the others were singing along.

She forced a *why-not* smile on her lips and followed the new pattern. Felicity was rocking it out with the women who'd led the way. Who knew she'd lighten up that much? Possibly the free-flowing champagne had done the trick.

Laughing, smiling, embracing people surrounded her, but the night felt empty. Every muscle in her body and face mannequin-stiff, she'd smiled during dinner and the toasts. She managed to choke down some of the crab-cake appetizer and a few bites of the beef medallions, but her stomach rebelled at more. Her napkin hid her slice of wedding cake until she slipped it onto a tray.

The only tears she'd allowed were for happiness during Thomas and Cleo's first dance and for the reconciliation with her dad. If she concentrated on that and on his amazing news, she'd smile and mean it. He and a woman named Nadia, who worked in the same Pentagon department, were an item. Serious, he said. She was "the friend" who'd encouraged him to talk to his daughter. Pressed for more answers, he promised to bring Nadia for a visit when the honeymooners returned home. Andie couldn't wait to meet the woman who'd softened the Old Man.

The dance troupe made another turn, giving her a three-sixty of the ballroom. No sign of that rat bastard

Pagano. Probably outside, like last evening. Fine, as along as she didn't have to see him again. His betrayal, like glass shards, cut deep.

She'd kicked off her heels a while ago, but her feet hurt anyway. On the last turn, she nearly tripped over her own feet. Dancing relieved some of her tension, but she couldn't keep up the happy façade much longer. When the song ended, she begged off, pointing to her feet. On her way to order a sweet tea, she waved at a DSF operative, one of several sprinkled among the guests.

"Here you go, sweet thing, just what you need. You look parched." The man Mimi had headed off by pulling Andie into line dancing slid a highball glass along the bar to her. Cleo's just-divorced and on-the-hunt uncle— fifteen years Andie's senior—waggled his bushy eyebrows at her. "I'll order myself another."

Dammit, why did people keep shoving drinks at her? She stared at the ice cubes shining in the amber liquid. She dipped her head and sniffed. Bourbon, probably the bar brand. Easy. It would be so easy to let it help her forget, to let it numb the pain oozing from her pores. But those effects would be fleeting and lead only to more grief.

She lifted her head and stared into the mirror behind the bar. If life hurt, it was better to feel pain than to feel nothing at all. Never again would she cocoon herself in a haze. She was in control. She was in charge of herself.

She slid the condensation-dappled glass back to him. "Thanks, but no thanks. I don't drink alcohol. Please excuse me." She couldn't stay there any longer. If he argued with her or pressed the drink on her, she'd dump it on him, consequences be damned.

Eyebrows leaping toward his receding hairline, he

gawped. "But, Andie—"

A flash of white that smelled of roses appeared from nowhere. "Hey, Uncle Randy, I need to drag my BFF away. You having a good time?"

He bobbed his head, but stayed mute, yielding without complaint.

Although Andie suspected what was coming, she let herself be pulled away by Cleo to an empty corner away from the music and conversation.

****

Mike kept to the shadows on the veranda, but couldn't stop his gaze from following Andie on the dance floor. In that dress that hugged every curve, curves he'd held close last night, she shimmered like heat lightning. Dammit, even with razor wire knotting his gut, watching those long legs flashing and her hips swaying turned him on.

Her face was a pale mask, a taut smile pasted on. She held her arms tight against her body in an air of exhaustion. Or hurt. He could barely restrain himself from marching in there and carrying her off so he could fix it between them. But all he could do was stand around with his thumb up his butt.

Looked like she had the same effect on that oily bartender Steve Sawyer. The asshole couldn't take his eyes off her.

Mike's interview with him hadn't yielded much, except a hinky feeling about the guy.

Sawyer projected a candid and willing attitude. Mike had run into guys like that before, so he knew a con job when he saw one. Saw the cracks in that gleaming shell. Faced with Mike's barely concealed hostility, Sawyer should've been nervous. He wasn't. He looked

83

Mike in the eye without fidgeting and spoke with a steady voice. He nodded and agreed in an ingratiating manner that was patently false.

Mike paced in a tight circle, rolled his shoulders, studied the half moon. Was he fooling himself? If he was honest, was he letting jealousy filter his perceptions? Shit, he couldn't be objective and do his job where Andie was concerned.

When he looked back into the ballroom, she was no longer dancing, but huddled in a corner with Cleo for what looked like a serious gabfest. And the smarmy bartender? Watching them with narrowed eyes and a tight mouth.

Enough. Mike needed the deeper background on Sawyer that he'd requested earlier.

Brick answered his call on the first ring. "Good. It's you. Get up here ASAP. You need to see this."

****

"What's wrong? Is it Mike?" Cleo said.

Andie mustered a smile that felt like it would crack open her face. "Nothing's wrong. I'm having a great time. This is a fabulous party. Didn't you see me kicking up my heels?"

"Uh huh. I also saw a woman holding herself together by a thread. If you were glass, you'd have shattered." Cleo hugged her close. "But I also saw a determined and brave woman who faced down temptation like an old-time gunslinger. I'm proud of you, hon."

"Thanks. Coming from you, that means a lot." Andie stopped at that. No downer delivery from her, not on Cleo's wedding day. "But I'm fine, really. Just tired. And my feet hurt."

Cleo's raised eyebrow and fixed stare meant she was prepared to wait out Andie's stonewalling.

Andie hugged her back, holding on for a long moment. She never could keep anything from Cleo.

"Yes, yes, it's Mike, that rat bastard." She told Cleo everything. The words tumbled out of her, raising her temperature to volcanic all over again. "He said my past didn't matter, that he was with me because he wanted to be. All so he could get me in bed." She dragged in a shaky breath. "Did you know about the art thieves' plot and that Thomas assigned Mike to protect me?"

"Thomas told me about the plot last night and why his people are really here. I reamed him out about keeping it from me. And from you and everyone else." Her lips curved in a soft smile. "He apologized sweetly."

"And about Mike?"

"That little fact, he failed to mention." Cleo smoothed the rumpled satin on Andie's shoulder. "Thomas can be dense about some things, but he recognizes as well as I do that you and Mike are attracted to each other."

"My brother the matchmaker? You're dreaming."

"It's a stretch, I know, but wouldn't you have thought it odd if it had been Brick or Hakim hanging around you?"

Andie hiked a shoulder. "Maybe. They're married with kids, and they think of me as the company mascot."

"And Mike sure as hell does not. Ask yourself what you'd have done if he'd fessed up last night that you were his assignment." As the band played a few attention-getting chords, Cleo grinned. "Gotta go. Time to toss the bouquet. You coming?"

"Hardly in the mood. Okay?"

Cleo winked. "No prob. I'm aiming the toss at Mimi. Think about talking to Mike. If his feelings for you are real, he's hurting now too." Picking up her skirts, she hurried away.

Andie sank onto a chair and hugged herself. She was replaying the confrontation with Mike in her mind when she noticed Mimi still at the bar.

Oh no, she would miss the toss. Andie started toward her, but stopped when Trudy beckoned to her daughter.

Mimi's hands went up in a *stop* signal to the barman. Grinning, Steve spoke, swiped an index finger along his nose, and aimed it at her. Something about his gesture seemed familiar, but maybe just a déjà vu kind of thing.

Andie stared at the floor as she searched her memory.

Not déjà vu. She recognized that gesture. Or had heard about it. Hairs rose on the back of her neck.

Chapter Nine

THE BOUQUET DROPPED into Mimi's outstretched arms. Applause erupted. Behind the group of women, a blushing Lucas scratched his chin and Max clapped him on the shoulder.

Andie removed her phone from her evening bag. That gesture, the figure by the nose, and the chin cleft. He could be *that* Steve. But why? She had to know.

Needing to get away from the noise of the party, she slipped out a side door. The veranda floor was cool on her bare feet as she padded around the building.

Voices singing along to "Don't Stop Believin'" followed her as far as the dark area where Thomas was attacked. She considered moving farther away, but the full moon and her phone provided enough light.

No calls or voice mail, dammit. Either Erin was ignoring her, or something was wrong. Or both. Her roommate had issues. Heck, so did a lot of people who went into social work, herself a case in point. Abused as a child, Erin found it hard to trust. She blew even small slights way out of proportion. Andie had talked her off the ledge more than once.

Much like Cleo advised Andie tonight. Crap.

She selected Erin's number. One more try, and then what? Confront Steve? But about what? That she suspected he was Erin's boyfriend who used to tend bar in Annapolis? No big whoop if it turned out he simply needed the extra money working a wedding.

"Hey, Andie."

Andie started at Erin's voice. Finally. "What's the matter? Why haven't you answered my calls?"

"As if you didn't know." A snort into the receiver. "I answered this time to tell you I'm moving out."

The angry tone shocked Andie. She couldn't imagine what she'd done to warrant her roommate packing up. "Tell me what you think I did."

"Only stole my boyfriend. Don't deny you've spent the weekend with Steve at that fancy wedding. Explains why I wasn't invited."

Was this only about not being invited to the wedding? Andie had explained more than once that the guest list was limited to personal friends and family of the bride and groom. The roommate of the groom's sister didn't count.

And Steve? Why would Erin think he'd left her for Andie? Erin had never brought him to the apartment or even showed her a photo. All she knew was he was a bartender, handsome, and older than Erin, who was thirty-one like her.

Andie rubbed her prickling nape with her free hand, whacking her ribs with the dangling bag. She winced. Damn metal. Calming her breathing, she spoke slowly and gently. "What does Steve look like?"

"What are you trying to do to me?" Erin's voice rose in pitch. She sounded as taut as wire.

"It's important. Please believe me. He's not my date. Send me his photo from your phone."

"He wouldn't let me take his picture. Superstitious, he said. In case I sneaked a shot, he sometimes checked my phone. He saw your picture, that one of you and me at the Spy Museum."

Andie's pulse jumped. He knew what she looked like, who she was. "Okay, so what does he look like?"

Erin sniffled. "Short brown hair, green eyes. So green I thought he wore colored contact lenses, but he doesn't. Very sexy cleft in his chin. And he wears this great cologne that smells like vanilla, as if you don't know. Is that enough?"

Add all that to the familiar gesture Erin had described to her more than once—on a little squeal—and it was more than enough. "Why do you think I know him?"

Silence, then a ragged sigh. "He kept asking about you, about the wedding. All kinds of details, where it was, the events. Like he was going there. With you. And then he broke up with me Thursday. Over the phone." Her voice broke, liquid with tears. "When I tried to call him later, I got the not-in-service message. His boss at the bar said he quit."

"Look, I'm really sorry about Steve and you, but I didn't steal him. I think he's the bartender here at the wedding reception. I have to hang up. I'll call you back when I find out what's going on." Before Erin could say anything more, Andie ended the call.

Steve's being at the inn was no longer just odd or a coincidence.

She stared at the speed dial icon for Mike. His words came back to her. *"Call me for anything that seems off."*

Where *was* Mike? Not out here as she'd imagined. She heard only a sleepy bird call and could see little in the dark. No lights in the wedding tent. Even the moonlight showed no one, none of the DSF guys. That didn't mean they weren't here. Protection at a distance, isn't that what she wanted? Her chest tightened, and she rubbed her sternum to ease the twinge.

She touched the icon. Lifted her finger. Lowered it.

That whisper of danger scraped the back of her neck again. Tension vibrated along her arms. Much as it pained her to talk to Mike, she had to make the call.

A large hand covered her mouth and yanked her backward. She slammed against a hard body smelling of alcohol and sweat. And vanilla cologne.

Steve.

Her heart thundered white noise in her ears, and she gasped for breath. How did she give herself away? He must've noticed her reaction to his finger-swipe gesture and her dash from the ballroom with her phone.

Which was still in her hand. Her heart jolted. *Mike!*

Cold metal bit into her neck. She had time to register that it was a pistol before he lowered his arm and whacked the phone away. It tumbled soundlessly across the grass and came to rest beneath a shrub.

Her mouth went dry as a cotton ball, and acid pain racked her chest.

She'd waited too long to make the call. No one knew where she was. Her mind flashed on the terror of her kidnapping last fall. Oh God. She heard herself whimper and gritted her teeth against the weakness.

"Don't make a sound or it'll be your last." The pistol dug into the soft place just beneath her chin. He took his hand from her mouth and, pressing her folded arm against her body, clamped her to his side. "I can't let you ID me, bitch. Walk."

****

In Brick's room, Mike sat down at a laptop. He'd

left Andie at the reception, in good hands. Other operatives would safeguard her and the other family members. After last night's attack, Devlin had called in more personnel. But still, unease about her safety niggled at him as he read Research's urgent report.

Steve Sawyer was an alias. His identity—Social Security, driver's license, job record—went back only ten years. The Social belonged to a man who died twenty-five years ago.

Mike and Brick donned flak vests with gun holsters, then shrugged into their suit coats. After alerting the other operatives and collecting equipment, they took the elevator. Fortunately no other hotel guests joined them.

Mike smoothed his pants leg, making sure the ankle holster didn't show. "The guy calling himself Sawyer should still be mixing drinks."

"I'll get Hakim to confirm that." Brick took out his phone. "No sense in showing ourselves and spooking him. We can have the manager call him into the back."

The doors whooshed open to the lobby as Mike's phone played the song he'd set as Andie's ringtone, Springsteen's "Dancing in the Dark." A chill feathered along his spine. She was so pissed at him, this had to be important. "Gotta take this."

Brick only nodded, listening to his own phone, as they stepped out.

"Andie, what is it? Are you okay?"

No reply. Only a faint whisper. A breeze or Andie?

Now his pulse was rioting. He cradled the phone in both hands. "Andie, answer me. What's going on?"

Still nothing. Only the light noise.

Where was she? The green blip located her outside on the veranda. No, just beyond the veranda. "Brick!

Andie's in trouble. Tracker has her outside."

Beside him, the team leader nodded. "Hakim, signal the others. Find the asshole now!" He turned to Mike. "Sawyer's disappeared. Manager didn't see him leave."

He kept the line open, just in case she started talking. They raced outside, following the green blip's coordinates.

Mike scanned the veranda and nearby area. Brick's flashlight beam swept across the lawn. The light breeze carried the scent of the river.

No Andie. Nobody at all.

Silence, except for the rustling of leaves and the frantic pounding of his heart.

He clicked End Call and called her back.

The strains of "I'm Still Standing" floated from beneath a nearby shrub.

****

Andie stumbled and tripped, letting her knees give way. If she could free herself, even for a moment, it would be just long enough to yell bloody murder. The jerk yanked her upright as if she weighed nothing. He slapped her hard across her face.

Pain exploded, cymbals clanged in her head. She would've fallen if he hadn't grabbed her again.

She hardly recognized the man who held her. The flirtatious barman veneer was gone, replaced by a hard-eyed, grim-faced thug. He wouldn't shoot her here. No silencer. Maybe it wouldn't fit beneath the bartender vest. Why was he doing this? He had to be part of the art theft gang.

What could she do? *Think!*

She gasped for breath and banked down the shudder that racked her. "You can't get away with this. Let me

go. People will be looking for me." *Mike, Thomas…
please.*

"Shut up." He hustled her around to the inn's far
side.

He marched her past the lot where she'd left her car
and to the employee parking lot beyond.

Her head pounded and rocks bit into her bare feet as
they lurched across the gravel. Someone had to see them,
someone going home after work.

Anyone. Any delay.

Andie stumbled again, part pain, part stalling. She
had to give Mike time to find her. He must know by now
that she was missing.

He'd lied to her, but maybe he had no choice, and
maybe she'd hurt him too. He'd still protect her. He
would look for her.

He *had* to come.

Steve dragged her down another row of vehicles.
The back of this lot was darker, secluded, too far away
for anyone to hear her if she screamed. If she could get
enough air past the tightness in her chest. She took a
shuddering breath against the icy fear sleeting through
her veins.

She couldn't let him take her away.

"Leave now. You'd get away before I could get
help. Besides, your hit man failed."

He uttered a contemptuous snort. "He was only a
decoy."

A decoy? What did he mean? That wasn't the real
attack? "If you hurt me, they'll find you and stop you."

He laughed, a nasty bleat. "Can't stop anything now.
The honeymoon will be a blast."

A blast? Her mind scrambled with the realization

that he didn't mean it figuratively.

The brake lights on the car ahead flashed.

The trunk lid popped open. Raising it higher, he shoved her closer. "Get in."

She stared into the black interior.

"No, you can't!" She yanked against his hold, but his grasp was as unyielding as steel. She twisted harder, pivoting her body away from his.

"Bitch! I should shoot you now."

Someone would hear the shot. She counted on his knowing that.

When he twisted with her and swung the pistol at her head, she ducked and kept turning.

They turned back and forth in a mockery of dance moves until they were side by side, their backs to the open trunk.

If she let him shove her in there, she'd die. And Cleo and Thomas would die.

What could she do? She had no weapons, not even the spike-heeled wedding shoes.

He held her only by her right arm. As she lowered her left, the evening bag's chain slid downward. She closed her fingers around it. In her pain and dread, she hadn't felt the bag's weight.

Steve pulled on her arm and started shoving her backward with his gun hand.

For a long second the world stopped, and then her heart hammered hard enough to break a rib. Adrenaline pumped through her entire body.

He might shoot her, but not yet. She gripped the slender chain.

And swung.

****

Not knowing if Andie was all right burned acid in Mike's nerves. His gut heaved. If that asshole hurt her… He clutched her phone and forced away tension so he could function.

He scanned the area beyond the inn. No lights, no movement.

"Let's go." Brick stowed his phone. "Best bet's his car. Back of the employee parking lot. 2008 Ford Crown Victoria. I'll tell you the rest as we go."

They took off running around the inn.

Crown Vic. Likely an old Police Interceptor model. If he'd already driven away, he'd be hard to catch.

But Mike would bet Andie was putting up a fight.

As they made it to the driveway between the guest lot and the employee one, Brick told Mike that Hakim was marshaling the rest of the DSF personnel, sending some to set up a roadblock, and calling the county cops.

A shot rang out.

Mike's blood ran cold, and he sprinted across the gravel toward the sound.

As he spotted the Crown Vic, Brick's hand on his arm pulled him up short.

The two men split up. Mike drew his Glock and crouched behind a sedan while Brick knelt behind another vehicle.

Sawyer appeared to have fallen backward into the open car trunk.

One hand kept a tight grip on Andie's arm and the other held a pistol. Maybe a 9mm. Hard to tell so far away from the safety lighting. He waved the gun around in an apparent effort to lever himself upright, but he met with little success because Andie was whacking him with her purse.

Was Sawyer's face bloody, or was it a trick of the light?

The angle was too awkward for Mike to chance a shot. He could hit Sawyer in the leg, but that would still let the asshole shoot Andie. Or, worst case, Mike might hit Andie.

While speaking quietly into his phone, Brick gave Mike the hand signal to go on point.

Crunching gravel on both sides of the lot alerted him. His glance found Hakim on his left and Max on his right.

"Sawyer," Mike yelled. "Put down your gun and let the woman go."

Still pounding on the hand gripping her, Andie turned toward him, relief on her beautiful face. She looked frantic and disheveled, but otherwise okay. *Hang on, sweetheart.*

He fixed his gaze on Sawyer, who'd gone still, as if calculating his next move.

"Led be go or I'll shood her."

His voice sounded strange, like he had a cold. He raised up a little, enough to make himself a bigger target.

"You can't get away. The road is blocked." Mike raised his pistol. "Drop the gun beside the car and let the woman go."

Sawyer raised his pistol toward Andie.

She swung the bag in a wide arc.

Metal connected with metal in a resounding crack, and the pistol flew out of his hand. It landed on the gravel and skidded away.

Sawyer lost his grip on Andie, and she fell forward onto her knees.

Before Sawyer could climb to his feet, Mike and

Brick rushed forward and hauled him out. Brick pushed him face down on the gravel, and Mike cuffed him with zip ties.

Max scooped up Andie and carried her off to the side.

Their prisoner turned his head. Blood smeared his jaw and trickled from his nose. "Bidge broke by dose!"

"I wish she'd broken more than your nose, asshole," Mike said. The knuckles on the man's left hand were bloodied and raw, thanks to Andie's metal barrel bag. Good.

Chuckling, Hakim helped Sawyer to sit up.

Another operative hustled over to Andie with a first-aid kit.

Mike bent over, propping his hands on his knees. He shook as the adrenaline drained from his muscles. He thought he knew fear, the way it clawed your throat and curdled your insides, but fear in battle had never prepared him for the sick horror of knowing a killer had snatched Andie.

Drawing a deep breath, he hustled over to where she stood with Max. Draped in his suit coat, she looked small and vulnerable. A welt on the side of her face was turning purple, and her fancy hairdo was only a memory, but otherwise she was whole and strong. His mama tiger had somehow gotten the better of the asshole. Not *his* mama tiger, but now maybe he'd have a chance to make it true.

If she'd listen to him.

"It's over, thanks to you," he said. "You ever want to try out for the Olympics, the hammer throw is your event."

Her hand went to her throat, and her mouth curved in a tremulous, fleeting smile. "Thanks. But it's not over.

Sawyer planted a bomb on the *Prowler*."

Mike's adrenaline spiked again. "Explain."

"That's all I know. He said the honeymoon would be a blast." Her gaze glittered with tears. "He was going to kill Thomas and Cleo. Oh…"

He started to go to her, but she wouldn't welcome his touch. Aside from being pissed at him, she was all folded inside herself at the moment. The aftermath of nearly being stuffed in a trunk.

And then Max wrapped his arms around her, breaking Mike's unprofessional lapse from dealing with the bomb.

Brick's voice brought his head up. "I heard. County bomb squad's been alerted."

A rush of voices and the scuff of shoes announced the arrival of Mike's boss and Cleo and Admiral Devlin. Max slipped his jacket away and stepped aside.

They surrounded Andie with hugs and exclamations of relief. Mr. D swept his sister into his arms and strode off toward the inn. With Andie's family to take care of her, she'd be fine.

Mike watched as they carried her to the inn. Dealing with the bomb, the scumbag in cuffs, the police—sirens were fast approaching—would take most of the night.

A night he'd rather spend apologizing to Andie.

Chapter Ten

AFTER THE DETECTIVE finished with her statement and left, Andie propped her legs on the cocktail table and admired her new footwear. Her brother's white cotton athletic socks nearly reached her knees.

Thomas and Cleo had insisted on taking her to their suite. Cleo provided an ice pack for Andie's bruised face, and bandages and ointment for her scraped feet and knees. When she wailed about grass stains and dirt ruining Cleo's sunrise design on the gorgeous dress, her friend declared she'd give her the original painting.

They hovered as if they felt responsible and kept exclaiming how she'd saved their lives and maybe those of others who might have been nearby when the bomb blew. Andie hadn't known what to say other than muttering that she'd just happened to prod Steve into blurting that information.

Beside her on the couch, her BFF squeezed her hand. "You okay now?"

"I am. Really, I'm fine. You don't need to worry about me... *Mom*."

Cleo huffed, but smiled and subsided.

And yes, Andie was fine. Mostly. When Mike had first rescued her, his unwavering gaze kept her steady, but when everyone crowded around, blocking her from him, the whole thing crashed down on her, and she was a shaking mess. Recounting the experience for the detective's recorder, from learning how Steve had set out to bartend the wedding to abducting her at gunpoint, drained most of her shock and terror, and she felt normal. Sorta.

Except for not knowing what to do about Mike.

She'd made such a fool of herself, why would he want her now? If he ever really did. Her ribcage felt too small and tight around her heart, and she let a weary sigh leak out.

What she needed was to be down the hall in her room, where she could think, and where she didn't have to keep reassuring her family. But they insisted she stay with them at least until the bomb was removed.

Thomas walked out of the bedroom, phone in hand.

"Any news? Have they defused the bomb?" she asked.

"Not yet. They've completed a thorough search and found only one device. C-4—that's plastic explosive—and a timer, on one of the engines." He looked up from the screen, a satisfied expression in his gaze. "Cops are allowing Brickley and Pagano to assist because of their history on the art theft case." He grinned. "Provided they don't interfere."

Andie set down the ice pack and sat up straighter. "And the news is?"

Thomas explained that fingerprints had identified the bartender/hit man as Stephen Ordman, who'd been arrested four years ago in connection to the murder of a Chicago mob boss. He was never charged and then disappeared. Probably a paid hit man, then like now. But he lawyered up so the detectives got no more out of him.

If the cops found his prints on the bomb, he'd face an attempted murder charge on top of assault and battery, threatening with a deadly weapon, false identification, and probably more. The long list of charges against him meant he wasn't going anywhere.

Once Norman Torres, who'd tried to knife Thomas, learned that Ordman was in custody, he was eager to tell all. Torres was initially paid fifteen grand to hang around and look suspicious as well as decoy the Devlin operatives so Ordman could plant the C-4.

"Funny thing." Thomas paused, his gaze flickering between them. For dramatic effect, a tactic Andie knew well. "When Torres let the air out of my tires and set off the alarm on my phone, Ordman couldn't board the *Prowler* because a woman was on board. You wouldn't know anything about that, would you, Andie?"

Her cheeks heated. "That was probably me. I sat on the boat for a while. I did see a man run down the lawn from the inn and turn around." Andie didn't know about the tires. That must've been when Mike received that emergency call and ordered her inside. *Crap*. Her chest tightened more painfully. "But then Torres had to distract the operatives again. The knife attack?"

"Right." He crossed the room and squatted beside her. "I see that look on your face. You are not, I repeat, not to blame yourself. Mike stopped the knife attack, and I wasn't hurt. They'd have planted the bomb earlier, is all. And it's my fault for not letting you know about the threat—" he cast a sheepish glance at his new wife, who blew him a kiss "—I wanted all of you to enjoy the weekend without worry. So chill." His eyebrows lifted meaningfully.

"Chillin', Tommy." Her brother, always a protector.

If he perceived she was still struggling with something, he'd probably think it a reaction to the attack. She reckoned next week she'd check in with her therapist. "Do you know any more?"

He rose to his feet and again examined his phone. "Ordman lifted the kitchen knife and pushed Torres to jump me. He wasn't supposed to actually connect, but he refused to do it at all unless he got paid ten grand more."

Thomas went on, explaining that the decoy's wife was wheelchair bound after a stroke and he was out of work. He got linked up with Ordman by his cousin, who happened to be head of the art-theft gang.

"So it is the art thieves!" Cleo exclaimed. "They hired Steve the hit man, who hired Torres as decoy. They really wanted you out of the picture."

"Seems Torres didn't realize being an accomplice would dump him in so much trouble. He's disgusted with himself and is giving up names and locations. Since the art thieves are behind the plot, FBI Art Crimes is taking both men off the local cops' hands. Maybe I can influence the prosecutor to go easy on him."

"What about Torres's wife?" Andie asked. "Can we get her some help, like a home care worker?"

Cleo hugged her, and Thomas said, "I'll see about it before we leave in the morning." His phone dinged. After studying the screen for a moment, he grinned. "Bomb's defused and removed. Head of the bomb squad said impressions on it look like fingerprints."

"It's been a long night. Now there's a giant understatement for you. It's almost daylight." Andie pushed to her feet, which stung, but who cared. She picked up the plastic bag holding her keys and lipstick. The detective had taken her battered metal bag as evidence. She didn't want it back, she told him, not with the hit man's blood smearing it.

She waved her hand as if it held a magic wand. "My work here is finished. Carry on with the honeymoon and the happily ever after."

****

Mike rubbed his nape as he neared Andie's room. The newlyweds had checked out and were busy moving luggage onto a hastily chartered cabin cruiser. The *Prowler* was still being processed as a crime scene. Andie wasn't there or in the dining room, and her car was still in the lot, so she had to be here.

He swiped his damp palms down his jeans and raised one fist. Tapped gently. Waited.

Nothing. And then a shadow crossed the security peephole.

He knocked again. "Andie, I know you're in there. I need to talk to you. Don't you want to know what the police found out?" If he could get inside, she'd have to listen to him.

"I already know all that. Thomas told me. Go away."

"I have your phone, remember?"

"Give it to Cleo. I'll get it from her."

"I can't. They're on the charter boat."

"I'll manage without. I don't want to talk to you." Her voice sounded very small, like her resistance was wavering.

Maybe it was too soon, and he should let her cool down.

No, he had to try. He pulled the leather case from his pocket and selected a tool. After they talked, he'd leave, give her time to think about it.

A faint click, and the lock gave. If the deadbolt and

103

chain were on, he'd talk to her through the door. He didn't freakin' care if every guest on the floor heard.

He turned the knob.

Chapter Eleven

MIKE HELD HIS breath and pushed. The door swung inward, and he stepped inside.

Dressed in the same tee and yoga pants that turned him on the other night, Andie stared open-mouthed. Her hair fell to her shoulders in remnants of the curly 'do. Hands planted on her hips, she backed around her suitcase, which sat in the middle of the room.

Packed up and ready to leave. He'd made it here in the nick of time, or he'd have missed this chance.

She narrowed her eyes. "What the hell? How did you do that?"

He slid the tool back into its slot. "Official Devlin Security Force lock-pick kit." He'd persuaded Brick to authorize its use.

"And you can just un-pick it and leave." Her voice sounded less certain, less pissed.

He took her phone from his windbreaker pocket and laid it on the desk beside him. "Hear me out, and then I'll leave." *If you still want me to.* "You're angry with me, and I don't blame you. I should've told you the truth Friday night about being assigned to protect you. I screwed up, and I'm sorry."

She chewed her lower lip. "So why didn't you tell me?"

Damn, she was going to make him sweat through it.

"I started to, but I thought you'd be so mad, you'd refuse to have anything more to do with me. So how could I protect you? I hoped you'd understand when I finally confessed."

Something flickered in her eyes as if she was considering his excuse. "I might not have been as ticked off."

"Then it's a triple apology." He took a step closer.

She looked doubtful, but otherwise didn't react. "And I accept. Is that it?"

"Not by half. Everything I said about how I felt about you, about us, I meant. I want to see where our relationship can go. I still feel that way."

Her mouth contorted as if she'd just bit into a pickled egg, and she hugged herself. "Even after my stupidity?"

"You'll have to explain that." He took another step, putting him close enough to catch her scent.

"Whether you'd told me about your protection gig would've made no difference. I was dumb and reckless. I left the inn alone and got myself snatched."

The prickle on his nape warned him not to screw this up, but he needed time to think. "Would you mind telling me how that happened?"

"Oh, yeah. You wouldn't know that." She described her suspicions about the bartender and demonstrated the familiar gesture that triggered her phone call to her roommate. "I wanted to call you, but I hesitated too long. He must've realized I recognized him or something. Thank God the tracker led you to me."

"You knew about that?"

"I found it Friday morning. Thomas must've installed it."

"He did." He took a deep breath and dived in. "I wasn't on the veranda when you went outside because Brick called me upstairs to see the research report on the man we now know as Steve Ordman. Luckily your call did go through, or I might not have located you fast enough."

"The bastard would've shut me in the trunk."

Her fierce glower made him grin. "You were doing a damn fine job of holding him off. The other bartender sent us to the parking lot. But here's the thing. Suppose you'd phoned me right away, and suppose Brick and I had sat Ordman down and grilled him, and maybe the cops even arrested him."

She looked expectant, waiting for him to go on. Finally her eyes widened and one hand flew to her mouth. "The bomb. Thomas and Cleo kept telling me I saved their lives, but I kept thinking how stupid I'd been. If you'd been upfront about protecting me, you're right that I'd have pushed you away and put myself in danger." She shook her head. "Well, I did that anyway. I *was* stupid." Raw anguish filled her eyes, and her voice was soft, thready.

Tenderness sharp as a knife pierced his heart. "Not stupid, loyal. You were trying to do what you said—make sure the wedding was perfect. And it was. And by taking that risk, you saved their lives." He had to tell her the rest. He'd put it off as long as he could. Any longer and she wouldn't believe him. She might not, even now.

An ache threatened to crush Andie's chest.

He was so gorgeous, even with fatigue bracketing his eyes and the scruff of beard darkening his jaw. He was honorable and strong and kind. Was Cleo right that she'd hurt him? Did he come only to return her phone and report on Steve Sawyer/Ordman?

His expression hardened, his mouth drawing into a thin line. His arms and legs were rigid. Oh God, he did say he wanted to see where things could go between them, or was he really going to tell her it would never work? But wasn't that what she wanted? Not *wanted*, but... Her throat tightened.

"I understand how hard it was for you to overcome abuse and addiction. I need you to know how much I respect that struggle. My father and brother didn't make it."

His words, wrenched from somewhere deep inside, shocked the hell out of her. She reached out, then dropped her arm. "I'm so sorry."

"The car accident that killed my dad happened because he passed out and slammed into a stone wall. Mom tried for years to get him to go for help, AA or something, anything. He refused, kept saying he could handle it."

"And your brother? The youngest, you said."

"Yeah, Danny, two years younger than me. He fooled around for a while after school, then joined up, the Army, infantry. Got sent to Afghanistan when I was there. To numb the fear, the stress, he got into cocaine. Probably other stuff too. One day on patrol, he was so stoned, he wandered into a field and triggered an IED."

The pain in his gaze had her closing the space between them. "You started to tell me this the other night, but something stopped you."

He still looked grim, but something softened in his eyes. "Too hard to talk about. But telling you now is important."

Asking why could wait. "You blame yourself about

Danny."

"Hard not to at first, but when I look back, I know I tried. He told me more than once to butt out."

She pictured him the other night as the rehearsal party was ending. She'd never seen him drink alcohol. "The champagne. You didn't dump it out not because you don't like champagne. Because of your family, you don't drink."

"I have a new fave—sweet tea." One side of his mouth ticked up, flipping her pulse, but his humor morphed into something raw and needy. "I told you I wanted a relationship beyond this weekend. I do want that. You're afraid of taking a chance, but it's not me you doubt. You battled addiction and beat it. After all you've overcome, you're still afraid of taking a chance on yourself."

She opened her mouth to object, but he held up a hand.

"Friday afternoon you said to me that you wanted the wedding to go off without a hitch because Cleo and your brother risked their lives for you. Seems like they think you were worth that risk. So do I. That's what I came to say."

He removed a rectangular box from his jacket pocket. "For whenever you need a reminder of how smart and tough you are." He held it out to her. "I'll leave now."

She took the box and turned it around to the clear plastic front. Inside was an action figure dressed in scanty red, white, and blue armor. She looked up at Mike, but tears blurred her vision. "Wonder Woman."

He nodded and turned toward the door.

Everything he'd said swept through her mind on a

cleansing breeze. Was she so defensive that she'd jumped—no, *jetted*—to the wrong conclusion? Cleo was right about everything.

Andie wanted this man so intensely she couldn't put the depth of her feeling into words. Why was she resisting? Could she, should she…? Sniffing back tears, she hugged the Wonder Woman box to her.

"Mike, don't go."

His hand still on the doorknob, he turned. Was that hope in his eyes?

She rushed on. If she stopped, tears would drown her words. "This is the sweetest thing anyone has ever done for me. I'll cherish her forever and she'll be my reminder. Everything you said was true. Fear of myself, of taking risks. I've hurt you by not believing you. And I… I want you too, to see where this… *we* can go. If you still want to try."

With a trembling hand, she set Wonder Woman on her suitcase and waited.

"Andie," he gritted out.

And then he wrapped her in his strong embrace and kissed her. Her forehead, her damp eyes, and finally her mouth. It was a claiming kiss, deep and thorough, full of demand, and she kissed him back with a fierceness she couldn't name. The need for this man, this amazing man who wanted her in spite of her past and everything she'd done to push him away, welled up in her. She ran her hands around his hard-quilted torso, wanting to touch every part of him, to absorb his strength and belief in her and lock it in her heart.

She heard a low rumble and his lips left hers.

"Empty belly. Sorry." His smile ticked up again, this time with real amusement. "I showered but wanted to see you before you left." He looked down. "What was that?"

"No breakfast here either."

"I hear the inn has a killer Sunday brunch." He winced. "Sorry. But it'd be our first real date."

"Reckon I missed Thomas and Cleo leaving."

"I might've omitted something about that earlier. I saw them *on* the boat, but at the dock, so they could still be there."

She stepped into flip-flops and led the way to the elevator. Other guests pulling suitcases joined them, silencing their conversation, but Mike took her hand.

"If we go wave bon voyage, will you care if my brother sees us as a couple?" she said a few minutes later as they left the lobby.

"Too late for that. He's the one who put us together. I resisted the idea at first, but I no longer care that you're the boss's daughter. You've grown on me."

She'd resisted too, so she couldn't argue. They hurried across the sloping lawn. The charter boat remained moored, decorated with balloons and a printed sign, *Just Married*. All the wedding party, her dad, and Cleo's family gathered along the shore and on the dock.

When they neared the happy crowd, Cleo waved and tugged on Thomas's arm. Hard to tell if he smiled or frowned, but he did wave. From somewhere "We've Only Just Begun" was playing, and people held mimosas, so apparently the honeymooners weren't ready to set sail just yet.

After a very long time of merely holding on, Andie was happy. Mike's belief in her warmed her inside and out and made her feel she could face anything. Before they joined the others, she needed to say one more thing. "You already know I'm not an easy person. This relationship stuff is all new to me, but I'll give it my best shot."

"New to me too, sweetheart. I do like a challenge."

The music changed to Etta James crooning "At Last."

In front of her brother and her dad and her friends, Mike pulled her into his arms and kissed her.

The Musical Selections from *AT LAST*, in the order they appear in the novella:

ISN'T SHE LOVELY?
DANCING IN THE DARK (original, 1931)
IT'S IN HIS KISS
SAVE THE LAST DANCE FOR ME
DON'T STOP BELIEVIN'
CANON IN D, PACHELBEL (the wedding processional)
SIGNED, SEALED, DELIVERED
AT LAST
CAN YOU FEEL THE LOVE TONIGHT?
ENDLESS LOVE
OLD TIME ROCK AND ROLL
HURT SO GOOD
DANCING IN THE DARK (Bruce Springsteen)
DON'T STOP BELIEVING
I'M STILL STANDING
WE'VE ONLY JUST BEGUN
AT LAST (No one can sing it like Etta James.)

A word about the author...

Occasional bouts of insomnia led to Susan Vaughan's writing career. When she couldn't sleep, she made up stories to fill the long, dark nights. Her stories throw the hero and heroine together under extraordinary circumstances and pit them against a clever villain. Besides curling up with a good mystery or romance, Susan enjoys walking her dog, boating, traveling, and volunteering. A former teacher, she is a West Virginia native, but she and her husband have lived in Maine for many years. Susan is the author of 16 novels and one children's book. Find her at www.susanvaughan.com, where you can sign up for her newsletter or contact her, or at https://www.facebook.com/susanvaughanbooks.